"*Frankie & Bug* is uplifting, bittersweet, and **MAGNIFICENTLY LOUD IN THE HEART AND SOUL.**" —ANDREW KING, THE UNIVERSITY BOOK STORE (SEATTLE, WA)

"This book is **FOR THOSE STRIVING TO BE WHO THEY ARE,** not what others see. And for those standing in alliance beside them." —SUMMER DAWN LAURIE, BOOKS INC., LAUREL VILLAGE (SAN FRANCISCO, CA)

"This is a book about different kinds of family and different kinds of courage, and I think it **WILL RESONATE WITH MANY READERS.**" —TEGAN TIGANI, QUEEN ANNE BOOK COMPANY (SEATTLE, WA)

"*Frankie & Bug* is outstanding. **EASILY ONE OF THE BEST MIDDLE-GRADES I HAVE EVER READ,** and so what we all need to be reading right now!" —HEATHER HEBERT, CHILDREN'S BOOK WORLD (HAVERFORD, PA)

"Wow. Forman's first foray into middle-grade novels **PACKS AN ENORMOUS PUNCH.**" —ROBIN STERN, BOOKS INC., CAMPBELL (CAMPBELL, CA)

"*Frankie & Bug* is **A JOY TO READ!** In this deeply moving, funny, and engaging coming-of-age story, rising fifth grader Beatrice 'Bug' Contreras learns much in the summer of 1987, about friendship, prejudice, patience, and making real lemonade." —KATHLEEN CAREY, LITTLE BOOK HOUSE OF STUYVESANT PLAZA (ALBANY, NY)

"This is a **COMING-OF-AGE STORY, A FRIENDSHIP STORY, AND AN ALLY STORY.** Bug and Frankie teach us all to 'hurry toward justice' always, and never forget that there is more love than hate in the world." —JAMIE ROGERS SOUTHERN, BOOKMARKS (WINSTON-SALEM, NC)

"I simply cannot recommend this book any more highly, as children understand that love **TRANSCENDS** all else." —CANDACE ROBINSON, VINTAGE BOOKS (VANCOUVER, WA)

"Full of **COMPLEX** characters who read so authentically, and rich with the nuances of real life, family, and love." —SHOSHANA SMITH, FLASHLIGHT BOOKS (WALNUT CREEK, CA)

"My eleven-year-old son and I read this one together, and as with any of Gayle's books, it didn't disappoint. The friendship between Bug and Frankie is an **IMPORTANT** one, today more than ever when acceptance and kindness are often hard to find." —CHRISTINE ONORATI AND SON, ADRIAN, WORD BOOKSTORES (BROOKLYN, NY & JERSEY CITY, NJ)

"A **PITCH-PERFECT** book about friends and family—accepting them and loving them unconditionally." —BECKY ANDERSON, ANDERSON'S BOOKSHOP (NAPERVILLE, IL)

"Is there NOTHING Gayle Forman can't do? I believe *Frankie & Bug* **SHOULD BE REQUIRED READING** for kids, parents, and teachers!" —KATHLEEN CALDWELL, A GREAT GOOD PLACE FOR BOOKS (OAKLAND, CA)

"Frankie and Bug learn that life is not always fair, justice may take time, and families all look different. **A THOUGHT-PROVOKING**, heartwarming story!" —PAM PAGE, PAGES: A BOOKSTORE (MANHATTAN BEACH, CA)

"Just a **LOVELY** read." —DEBBIE BUCK, VINTAGE BOOKS (VANCOUVER, WA)

"The heart of this story is friendship, and the understanding each character shows for each other despite differences of age, identity, and ethnicity is **EXACTLY THE KIND OF LOVE AND COMPASSION WE WANT TO INSPIRE YOUNG READERS**." —TILDY LUTTS, BELMONT BOOKS (BELMONT, MA)

"An **EXCELLENT** fall read for kids nine to twelve years old." —MICHELE BELLAH, COPPERFIELD'S BOOKS (SEBASTOPOL, CA)

"Bug **SHOWS A WONDERFUL INNOCENCE,** reminding us adults that prejudice 'has to be carefully taught.' In the end, Bug, Frankie, and their whole found family pledge to 'hurry toward justice,' a pledge we all can and should make along with them." —KATE REYNOLDS, COLGATE BOOKSTORE (HAMILTON, NY)

FRANKIE
& Bug

GAYLE FORMAN

Aladdin

NEW YORK   LONDON   TORONTO   SYDNEY   NEW DELHI

ALADDIN

An imprint of Simon & Schuster Children's Publishing Division

1230 Avenue of the Americas, New York, New York 10020

First Aladdin hardcover edition October 2021

Text copyright © 2021 by Gayle Forman, Inc.

Jacket illustration copyright © 2021 by Angeles Ruiz

All rights reserved, including the right of reproduction in whole or in part in any form.

ALADDIN and related logo are registered trademarks of Simon & Schuster, Inc.

For information about special discounts for bulk purchases, please contact Simon & Schuster Special Sales at 1-866-506-1949 or business@simonandschuster.com.

The Simon & Schuster Speakers Bureau can bring authors to your live event. For more information or to book an event contact the Simon & Schuster Speakers Bureau at 1-866-248-3049 or visit our website at www.simonspeakers.com.

Book designed by Laura Lyn DiSiena

The text of this book was set in Alegreya.

Manufactured in the United States of America 0921 FFG

10 9 8 7 6 5 4 3 2 1

Library of Congress Cataloging-in-Publication Data

Names: Forman, Gayle, author.

Title: Frankie & Bug / by Gayle Forman.

Other titles: Frankie and Bug

Description: First Aladdin hardcover edition. | New York : Aladdin, 2021. | Audience: Ages 8 to 12. | Summary: In the summer of 1987 in Venice, California, ten-year-old Bug and her new friend Frankie learn important lessons about life, family, being your true self, and how to navigate in a world that is not always just or fair.

Identifiers: LCCN 2021003310 (print) | LCCN 2021003311 (ebook) | ISBN 9781534482531 (hardcover) | ISBN 9781534482555 (ebook)

Subjects: CYAC: Friendship—Fiction. | Family life—Fiction. | Transgender people—Fiction. | Salvadoran Americans—Fiction. | BISAC: JUVENILE FICTION / LGBTQ+ | JUVENILE FICTION / Family / General (see also headings under Social Themes)

Classification: LCC PZ7.F75876 Fr 2021 (print) | LCC PZ7.F75876 (ebook) | DDC [Fic]—dc23

LC record available at https://lccn.loc.gov/2021003310

LC ebook record available at https://lccn.loc.gov/2021003311

FOR **ISABEL**
AND HER ABUELITA
AND ALL THOSE SEARCHING
FOR THEIR PLACE IN THE WORLD

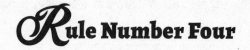

Rule Number Four

TEN DAYS BEFORE SCHOOL let out, Mama announced that summer was canceled.

She didn't say it straight out like that. But she might as well have. What she did say to Bug was: "What would you like to do this summer?"

This was a dumb question. Mama knew what Bug wanted to do this summer. The same thing she'd done for the last two summers, ever since Danny had persuaded Mama that there was no need to spend good money on the Y camp (which they both hated, Danny quietly so, and Bug noisily) now that he was old enough to watch them both all summer. For free.

"You can buy a new car instead," Danny had said. Clever of

him, Bug thought, because Mama was always complaining about the Datsun and its busted air conditioner.

So, after very elaborate negotiations with Phillip and Hedvig, their upstairs and downstairs neighbors who each sometimes watched Danny and Bug, and yet another consultation with Kip, the always-sunburned lifeguard who manned Tower 19, Mama had agreed to let them spend the summers alone. "With conditions," she said.

Conditions, Bug had soon discovered, was another name for rules. But conditions sounded nicer.

Mama typed the "conditions" onto a piece of thick, fancy paper she used at her job at the mayor's office. Then she made Danny and Bug both sign it. This, she explained, turned conditions into a contract.

The contract promised that Bug and Danny would:

1. Always go to Tower 19 and check in with Kip.
2. Always swim together if they went in past their knees.
3. Never touch so much as a toe in the water if the riptide flag was up.
4. Always stay together.

Rule number four was typed up in just the same way as the

others, but Mama repeated its importance so often that Bug understood it was the most important one of all. Bug was not generally fond of rules, even when they were called conditions, but this one, the idea that she and Danny must always, always stay together, well, she liked that one just fine. It made her feel safe.

The list had been taped to the refrigerator that first beach summer, and all that following fall and winter. In the spring, when Mama was doing her big cleaning, she had taken it down. But Bug had retrieved the paper from the trash and hung it back up. She'd told Mama it was because she might forget the rules this coming summer, but the truth was, the list had become a promise. The promise of summer.

For almost three years, the list had stayed on the fridge, fastened into place with a ladybug magnet. So when in the waning days of fourth grade, Mama asked what Bug wanted to do for the upcoming summer, the answer was obvious: "I want to go to the beach," Bug told Mama.

Mama got a funny look on her face, which in turn gave Bug a funny tickling in her stomach. Mama called this the Gut Voice and told Danny and Bug to listen to it. But Bug didn't want to listen to her Gut Voice, because what it was saying—even before Mama said, "I think we might need to change it up this summer"—was that summer was about to be canceled.

"Why do we have to change it up?" Bug wasn't entirely sure what "changing it up" meant, but she didn't want to ask, lest she look babyish. That was Danny's favorite insult as of late. And there was no way she would prove it true.

"It's just that Danny . . ." Mama stopped herself. "Daniel." *Daniel.* That was what Danny wanted to be called now. "Needs a bit of space this summer."

Bug had been hearing a lot about *Daniel's need for space* these past few months. First, early in the spring, Danny had told Mama that he didn't want to go to the magnet school he and Bug had both attended since kindergarten. This coming fall, he would be attending Venice High School.

A few weeks after that, Mama had taken Bug out for ice cream on the Santa Monica Pier and told Bug she was getting her own room. For a brief second, Bug had thought they were moving to one of those big houses with wall-to-wall carpeting and grassy backyards with pools, like the one her friend Beth Ann lived in. But then why would Mama be taking her out for ice cream to deliver good news? Ice cream was for bad news.

The bad news was this: Bug was being moved out of the biggest bedroom she and Danny had always shared and into a tiny alcove next to the bathroom that Mama had sometimes used as an office. It was too small to fit a bed and a dresser and desk, so with Hedvig's blessing—she was their landlady as well as their downstairs neighbor—Mama and Phillip built Bug a sleeping loft. Bug *did* like the loft. It had a wooden ladder and her window looked out onto a big magnolia that made it feel like she was sleeping in a tree house. But even if she liked the room okay, that didn't mean she wanted it. No one had asked if she wanted it. And worse, Danny got to keep the biggest room, instead of switching with Mama, who had the medium-sized room. It just wasn't fair! Bug had complained to Mama about this. Which was a big mistake. One thing about Mama was that she didn't give two hoots about fair.

And now, *Daniel's need for space* meant that Bug's summer was canceled. "It's just that Daniel," Mama was explaining, "has babysat you for the past few summers. . . ."

"Babysat?" Bug was offended. "Danny doesn't *babysit* me. In summer, we go to the beach. It's what we do."

"Well, this summer, we're going to have to figure out something else for you to do."

School had yet to let out, but Bug could feel the summer slipping through her fingers like sand at the beach, which she would not be going to.

She wanted to cry. Bug loved the beach. And the three months she got to spend there made all the bad parts of living in Venice—like her pretend bedroom and hearing gunshots at night and having to sit on a bus two hours a day to go to a good school and never having friends sleep over because nobody's parents wanted them to sleep in a place where gunshots went off at night—worth it. Bug loved everything about the beach: the way the brisk water made her toes go numb, the way the drying salt made her skin feel tight, the way tropical tanning oil smelled, and the way the sand sounded when you laid your head against it. She even loved things about the beach other people hated, like how saltwater stung her scratched mosquito bites, or how the sand got everywhere—and she meant everywhere, in her sheets, her shoes, in the crack of her butt.

Mama couldn't take that away from her. She just couldn't!

"I don't want to figure something else out!" Bug cried. "I want it to be like the other summers."

Mama shook her head. "Daniel is fourteen. He wants to hang out with friends his own age. I think that's fair."

"Fair?" Bug scoffed, feeling the heat in her earlobes, which was how she knew she was about to lose her temper. "What do you care about fair?" Because wasn't Mama the one who always told Bug,

"Life isn't fair—the most you can hope for is that it's just"?

Mama put a hand on Bug's shoulder. "I understand you're disappointed."

But Bug was more than disappointed. Because in that moment, she suddenly understood what *Daniel's need for space* really meant. It meant space away from Bug.

The realization made tears spring to her eyes. She blinked them back. She wasn't a baby. She was ten! But Mama saw. She stroked Bug's cheek, a gesture that made her feel even sadder, which in turn made her madder. She stomped her feet, and balled her fists, not even caring how immature this made her look.

"I know you're upset. I promise you'll have a fun summer." Mama took a breath. "At camp."

"No way. Nohow. I'm not going back to the Y camp." Y camp was the worst! You spent days inside in a moldy-smelling gymnasium, making lanyards or shaping clay into pots that never kept their shape. When you did go swimming, which was only twice a week, it was at an indoor pool. The ocean was just blocks away, but you had to swim in an *indoor pool*. It was the kind of thing Phillip would call a *travesty*.

"I'd rather stay with Hedvig!" Bug said, not because she wanted to spend the summer in their landlady's apartment, but just to show just how little she wanted to attend the Y camp.

Mama put on her thinking face. "If that's what you want, I'll ask." She paused. "Maybe you can stay some afternoons with her and others with Phillip when he's not working."

That *wasn't* what Bug wanted. Hedvig was okay, but her apartment, which took up the ground floor of their building, was full of junk, and all Hedvig did all day was watch soap operas. Phillip's apartment, which took up the top floor of their triplex, was much neater, and Phillip, when he was home, did much more interesting things, like make collages out of old *Time* magazines with Bug, or play songs on his baby grand piano. But neither Phillip nor Hedvig would take Bug to the beach. And the beach was the only place she wanted to spend her summer.

"Can't I go to the beach by myself?" Bug asked. "I'd check in with Kip. And only go up to my knees." The thought of not being able to dive headfirst into the waves made Bug sad, but not as sad as sitting home all summer. She would show Mama she could compromise.

"I'm afraid not."

"But you let Danny go alone with me."

"Daniel's a boy," Mama said.

"What's that got to do with it?" Bug could swim just as strong as Danny. She could stand the cold water just as long as Danny. She wasn't one of those girls who was scared of sand crabs or attacking seagulls.

"A lot," Mama said. "And you're only ten."

"I'll be eleven soon. And Danny was only twelve when we started going to the beach ourselves."

"You'll be eleven in *February*," Mama reminded her. "And I know two years doesn't seem like much, but there's a world of difference between ten and twelve." Mama shook her head. "I'm sorry, Bug. You can't go alone."

"I won't be alone. I'll have Bian and Duane and Randy and Zeus." These were Bug's summer friends, people she didn't see too much during the regular year when school kept her too busy to spend much time on the boardwalk but whom she saw every day as part of her and Danny's beach routine.

"I'm sorry," Mama repeated.

"No, you're not," Bug shot back. "Because if you were, you wouldn't be ruining my summer!" And then she could hold it in no longer. She burst into blubbering, babyish tears.

"I'm sorry, sweetie," Mama repeated. "I'll try to redeem your summer."

Bug thought these were just empty words, but a week later, when Mama told her that some nephew of Phillip's was coming to spend the entire summer in Venice, Bug understood, for better or for worse, whether she liked it or not, that *this* was her summer's redemption.

Frankie

HIS NAME WAS FRANKIE. He was eleven years old. And from Ohio. That was all anyone would tell Bug. Not if he liked the beach or knew how to roller-skate or ate fish and chips with tartar sauce, like Danny did, or vinegar and salt like Bug did. "You'll find out soon enough," Mama said when Bug peppered her with questions. This annoyed Bug. Frankie was being brought out here for her. Didn't she have the right to know these things?

Phillip was taking the day off from work to pick Frankie up from the airport, and he invited Bug to join him. "I suppose I'll go," she said, as if she hadn't spent the first few days of summer vacation bored out of her skull, commuting from their apartment to Hedvig's to the tetherball courts at the elementary school on the corner, which, according to the triangle map Mama had drawn, was where she was allowed to go alone. But Bug refused to show any enthusiasm about this Frankie, because once again, no one had even asked her what she thought.

Bug met Phillip at his parking spot in the alley behind their building. He was already cranking down the top to his car—a VW Rabbit convertible, which Phillip called the Cabriolet—because he knew that Bug *always* wanted the top down, even in winter, when it was so freezing Phillip had to blast the heater to keep Bug's teeth from chattering. He opened the glove box and pulled out the purple silk scarf he kept in there, special for her, tying it under her chin. "You look just like Grace Kelly," he said, same as always, even though Bug knew from old movies that Grace Kelly had straight blond hair and porcelain skin and Bug had frizzy brown hair and what Mama called olive skin, which confused Bug, because weren't olives green?

If she was half-excited to meet Frankie, Bug was whole-excited to pick him up at the airport. Though they lived less than ten miles from LAX, Bug had never been inside it. She'd never been on a plane. Never gone to the airport to greet anyone, because the only person who ever visited them was Aunt Teri, and she always took the Greyhound bus down from Visalia.

Airplanes fascinated Bug. She loved watching the jets take off over the Pacific. Danny had taught her how to follow their trajectory. If they turned around, Danny said, they were going to Chicago, or maybe New York, or maybe England, but if they carried on straight over the ocean, that meant they were going to Hawaii, or even all the way across to Japan or Vietnam, which was where Bian was from, though she hadn't come here on a plane but on a boat.

"Would you like to choose the music, Beatrice?" Phillip asked. That was another thing about Phillip. He did not believe in shortening names. He called Mama Colleen, never Co as other people did. He'd always called Danny Daniel. And he got grumpy if people called him Phil. "I am not a verb," he once told Bug. "And you, my dear, are not an insect."

Danny would probably set the dial to 106.7, KROQ, but Bug had seen Phillip make the same face to Oingo Boingo that Mama did when she balanced the checkbook. "The classical station is okay with me."

Phillip loved classical music. Whenever he listened in the car, he held the steering wheel with one hand and waved with the other. Like he was conducting. Bug wondered if he did that when he gave piano lessons to his students, some of whom, she'd heard him tell Mama, were so bad they made his ears bleed.

When the song ended, the announcer cut in. "We have breaking news. Investigators are now saying that the bludgeoning of an Arcadia woman in her home last night follows a similar pattern of several Southland nighttime home invasion murders that police are now attributing to a serial killer they're calling the Midnight Marauder."

"Marauder?" Bug repeated.

"Let's change the station, shall we?" Phillip said, moving the dial to KROQ. The deejays were talking, too, not about serial killers, but the upcoming July Fourth holiday.

"What do you get America for its two hundred and twelfth birthday?" one deejay asked. "Gin?"

"It's two hundred and eleven, you numbnuts," the other deejay said. "It's 1987 now."

"Izzit?" asked deejay number one. "I guess my last July Fourth party was a little too wild."

Phillip turned the radio off. The car crested above the wetlands of Playa del Rey. The ocean twinkled in the distance. Even from here, Bug could smell the briny scent, her favorite perfume. She missed the beach with a deep ache and wondered if Mama would take her and Frankie later. But then she remembered the announcement on the news about the Midnight whatever his name was. Mama's job with the mayor was in the press office, and when there were big stories, she had to work extra.

"Where is Arcadia?" she asked Phillip.

"Far away, Beatrice. Almost another city. Don't worry."

"Is it run by the mayor?" Bug wanted to know.

"I'm not sure. Why do you ask?"

"Because if it's run by the mayor, Mama will have to work late and won't take me and Frankie to the beach."

Phillip's mustache twitched upward as it did before he laughed, though Bug wasn't sure what was so funny. "We're almost there," he said as the road ran parallel to a runway. Overhead, a plane rumbled so close it made the car shake. The air filled with a strange but not unpleasant smell that Phillip said was jet fuel.

"Have you ever been on a plane?" Bug asked.

"Of course."

"How old were you the first time?"

Phillip paused to think. "I suppose that would be when I came out here from Ohio. I would've been twenty-four."

"When was that?" Bug asked.

Phillip gave her a quick glance, as if to say, *nice try*. That was another thing about Phillip. Though Danny and Bug had known him almost all their lives, though they had a key to his apartment, much about him remained a mystery. Like his age, for one. Bug had no idea how old he was. They never celebrated his birthday, even though he baked elaborate cakes for theirs with their ages decorated in frosting, except for Hedvig, who said at her age, she didn't need it advertised, so Phillip made up different ages for her each birthday. Last time she was nineteen.

"I remember landing," Phillip said, "and seeing the ocean for the first time."

"Because there's no ocean in Ohio?" Bug said, eager to show off her geography skills.

"Right, but we have Great Lakes, which look like oceans a little bit because you can't see to the other side and they have waves, but there's nothing that compares to the Pacific."

On that note, Bug was in complete agreement.

Frankie's flight was late, so Bug and Phillip wandered the airport, looking at the departure boards to see all the places the planes went: Chicago and San Francisco and Atlanta, even Mexico City! South past Mexico City was El Salvador, which was where Bug's father was from.

When Frankie's plane pulled into the gate, they waited for all the other passengers to get off before a stewardess finally came off with Frankie. At eleven, Frankie was a year older than Bug, but he looked younger: skinny, with knobby knees full of scabs, big ears sticking out of a short, choppy haircut that Bug recognized as a kitchen cut. (Bug and Danny had suffered through many such cuts until Phillip had taken over barbering duty, though recently *Daniel* had started going to some place on Washington, where they did lopsided new-wave cuts that Phillip refused to do.)

Phillip waved. Frankie walked over and they shook hands and then hugged.

Bug felt a sting of jealousy. Phillip might bake her cakes for her birthday and keep a Grace Kelly scarf in his car for her, but she couldn't remember a time when he'd hugged her.

"Welcome to California, Frankie," Phillip said.

"Thank you. It's nice to meet you," Frankie said solemnly.

"Wait! You've never even met?" Bug asked.

"I have not had the pleasure of meeting this handsome young man," Phillip said. "Frankie, this is Beatrice. Beatrice, this is Frankie."

"You can call me Bug. Everyone else does." But then she had a thought. "Is Frankie short for something? Because Phillip doesn't like shortening names."

Frankie looked at Phillip with wide, unblinking eyes. Phillip smiled and put a hand on his shoulder. "I'm lengthening Frankie's name, as Frankie is long for Frank," Phillip said firmly. "Let's go collect your bags, shall we?"

"This is all I brought," Frankie said, lifting his backpack. It was hardly bigger than Bug's school bag.

This for the entire summer? You needed multiple bathing suits, plus shorts for daytime and jeans when it got cold at night.

"I hope you brought more than one bathing suit," Bug said.

After a brief pause, Frankie replied, "I didn't bring any bathing suits."

"But how are we supposed to go to the beach if you don't have a bathing suit?"

Frankie looked confused. Bug was dismayed. Surely, someone must have told him that the point of his coming out to Venice for the summer was to keep her company, so she could go to the beach and not be alone.

"I don't like the beach," Frankie said.

Bug couldn't believe her ears. "But you've never been to our beach!" she countered. "The Pacific Ocean is nothing like your stupid lakes."

"Beatrice," Phillip said mildly. He turned to Frankie. "If that's all you have, we can head home." He placed an arm around Frankie's shoulders and the two of them started walking through the terminal, like they'd totally forgotten Bug existed. She counted to herself, wondering how many seconds before they realized she wasn't alongside them. She got to six when Phillip finally swung around. "Beatrice, coming?"

"You know we have a serial killer, right?" Bug announced as they rode the escalator down past the WELCOME TO LOS ANGELES sign. "He just killed again. We heard it on the radio."

"Beatrice," Phillip said, an edge of warning in his voice.

"He bludgeoned someone to death," Bug continued, even though she wasn't sure what *bludgeon* meant.

"That's enough, Beatrice!" Phillip said. "Let's give Frankie some time to settle in before we scare the bejesus out of him."

Scaring the bejesus out of him was exactly the point.

But Frankie didn't look scared. He just looked interested. Which wasn't the point. "I'll add it to my map," he said.

"What map?" Bug asked.

"Where all the Midnight Marauder attacks have happened."

"You know about the Midnight Marauder?"

"Yeah. It's been on the news. My dad didn't want me to come, but my mom said a deal was a deal. And anyhow, I have my map to keep track of all the places he's struck." Frankie tapped his backpack.

"You brought a map?" Bug asked. "With you?"

"Well, yeah," Frankie replied, like what kind of dummy *wouldn't* bring a serial-killer map when traveling to the place where a serial killer was on the loose? He said it like a *duh*. Which made Bug feel dumb, and then cross.

And that was when it hit her. This Frankie, who'd been sent here to redeem her summer, was going to ruin it even more.

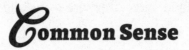

Common Sense

AS BUG SUSPECTED, Mama had to work late, so there was no time for the beach that afternoon. It also meant they all had to wait for Mama to get home to eat because Phillip had planned a special Welcome to Venice dinner for Frankie. Bug was already irritated enough about Frankie, who had not even packed a bathing suit, and now it was his fault she was hungry, too. By the time Phillip and Frankie knocked on the door, arms full of platters, she was in a full-on sulk.

"We're eating on the lanai," Phillip said, handing Bug and Danny each a platter to carry down. "Hedvig's joining us too."

"Great. I'm famished," Mama said, zipping up her jeans—which she always changed into after work—as she came out of her room.

"What's a lanai?" Frankie asked.

"You'll see," Phillip said.

They trekked downstairs, into and through Hedvig's ground-floor apartment, to the small patch of concrete nestled between the back of the building and the alley with the parking spaces where Mama and Phillip kept their cars. (Hedvig didn't have a car; even though she'd lived in Los Angeles more than thirty years, she didn't know how to drive!)

The area used to be an ugly chain-link-enclosed space where Hedvig stored her excess junk, but a few years ago, Phillip asked Hedvig if he could turn it into a communal backyard. Hedvig agreed, so long as they found a new place for her "treasures," so Phillip and Mama moved Hedvig's jumble to the shared hallway at the entrance of their building. Then Bug and Danny had helped Phillip put up a cedar fence inside the chain-link one and plant bamboo, bougainvillea, gardenias, and night-blooming jasmine in containers that Phillip made.

In summer, they often ate out here all together, which Bug mostly liked, except for one problem. Hedvig. Or more to the point, Hedvig's cooking.

"Stair-frey," she said, plunking down her contribution to the dinner in a cracked, dirty gray bowl that looked fresh from her junk pile.

Frankie just stared.

"She means stir-fry," Bug said, translating less because of Hedvig's Hungarian accent than her peculiar cooking. Stir-fry, at the Chinese Diner, was a bunch of vegetables mixed together in a yummy sauce. *Stair-frey* was when Hedvig tossed whatever was in her fridge—sludgy vegetables, glacially frozen meat, takeout of unknown origin—in a wok and coated it with Taco Bell hot sauce packets, which Hedvig hoarded.

Frankie's mouth hung open, just as it had on the drive back from the airport. Phillip had gone the long way home, showing Frankie the Marina del Rey with its fancy high-rises and sailboats, the Santa Monica Pier, with its carousel and bumper cars, before piloting the car back to the grittier streets of Venice, stopping along Speedway where the surfers, the skaters, the punks, and the tourists mixed together. "Never seen anything like this before, have you?" Phillip had asked Frankie with a twinkle in his eye.

By the way he was now gaping, Bug guessed Frankie had never seen anything like Hedvig before either. She was wearing an outfit she called resort wear—which was really just flouncy pajamas she wore day and night—and there were so many bangles jangling up and down her arms she had to push them down to bend her elbow. Most days she wore a turban because she didn't like how thin her hair now was, and stick-on eyelashes that sometimes didn't stick so well. Mama and Phillip both claimed Hedvig had been very glamorous and beautiful when she was younger, but Bug couldn't quite picture her any way other than how she was now.

"Lovely, Hedvig," Phillip said as he laid out platters of grilled shrimp, rice pilaf, salad, and cubed pineapple served in a carved-out shell because Phillip always did it special like that.

But Frankie stared at Phillip's platter of shrimp with the same perplexed expression he did the stair-frey. Danny, meanwhile, helped himself, hogging so many shrimp that Mama made him put a few back. He passed the plate to Frankie, who passed it to Mama without taking any. "They're really good!" Danny told him. "Your uncle's specialty."

Frankie's nose twitched as he stared suspiciously at the shrimp. "How are you supposed to eat them?"

"Wait, have you never had shrimp before?" Bug asked.

"I didn't eat much shellfish until I moved to the coast," Phillip told Bug. He turned back to Frankie. "Give them a shot. They *are* my specialty. And you eat the fleshy part and leave the tails."

"Like this!" Danny demonstrated.

"No, thank you," Frankie said.

"Have some stair-frey," Hedvig said, thrusting her bowl at him. "It is *my* specialty."

If Frankie had been at all nice to her on the drive back from the airport, Bug might've kicked him under the table to warn him about Hedvig's food. But not only had he insisted on having the top up, and stolen the front seat, he'd hardly spoken to her. So Bug kept her opinions to herself. If he barfed, it would serve him right!

"Phillip, you are such a good cook," Hedvig said, her mouth full of shrimp and rice. "Someone should marry you."

For the longest time, Bug hoped *Mama* would marry Phillip. After all, they did everything together, from eating meals to going grocery shopping to watching *Moonlighting* every Tuesday night. Who cared if Phillip was older? He was nice and funny and Bug wouldn't mind having him for a father. But on the few occasions Bug had suggested Mama and Phillip getting married, Mama had laughed harder than she had when they watched *Airplane!*

By the time they finished dinner, it was getting dark. Hedvig began hurriedly clearing the dishes.

"What's the rush? I bought an ice cream cake," Mama said. "From Carvel."

"Midnight Marauder," Hedvig said.

"I hardly think he's going to come after our dinner party," Mama said.

"Why? Does the mayor know something?" Hedvig asked, scraping Frankie's untouched stir-fry portion back into the serving bowl. "Do you have inside information?"

Mama's job at city hall was to tell reporters what was happening when there was news. This meant that when there was a big story—a tractor trailer overturned on the 405, a brush fire in Baldwin Hills—Mama often knew about it first.

"No, but I have common sense," Mama said. "He's nowhere near here. He's not going to bother us."

"Better safe than sorry." Hedvig picked up her still-full bowl. "Leftovers for lunch."

"Leftover leftovers," Bug heard Danny mutter softly under his breath. She would've liked to say something back—left *over* leftover leftovers—but that was the kind of thing she could do with Danny, not Daniel.

"I don't think we have to worry," Frankie piped up. "Almost all the murders have been after midnight."

"Is that true?" Bug asked Mama.

Mama shrugged, wearing what Phillip called her poker face, meaning her expression didn't give much away. Mama said she'd learned to do this because sometimes she didn't want the reporters she talked to knowing everything she did.

"Also," Frankie added, "he likes yellow two-story houses. This apartment building is gray shingled and has three stories."

By the surprised look on Mama's face, Bug knew this *was* true. She was begrudgingly impressed, not that she was going to let Frankie know that. Nor was she going to tell him that the news of the Midnight Marauder's preference for yellow two-story houses was reassuring.

After they all went inside, Bug pulled the dictionary down from the shelf and looked up *bludgeon*. She wished she hadn't. It took her a long time to fall asleep.

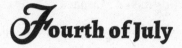

Fourth of July

PHILLIP WENT TO THE BEACH exactly two times each year. Once on New Year's Day, when he did what was called a Polar Bear Swim with a bunch of other guys. Bug did not get this. The water in January was freezing! The other time was on the Fourth of July, when Phillip accompanied Bug, Mama, and Danny to the beach. And even though the water was, if not warm, not freezing, Phillip didn't go in at all. Bug did not get this, either.

Bug was not sure if the tradition would continue this year, now that Danny had become Daniel and wanted nothing to do with her, and now that Phillip had a nephew, with whom he'd spent the past few days on outings Bug was not invited to, and now that the Midnight Marauder had started keeping Mama at work so much.

So she was relieved when she woke up on July Fourth morning to find Mama in the kitchen, wearing her crocheted bikini under a sundress, drinking coffee with Phillip.

"Did you make lunch?" Bug asked Phillip.

"Good morning to you, too," Phillip said.

"What'd you make?" When she and Mama and Danny went to the beach, they just packed peanut-butter sandwiches and sodas they bought at Dixon's, the market on the corner. But when Phillip came, they feasted. She saw the cooler on the counter and went to peek inside.

"Leave that closed," Phillip admonished, slapping her hand away. "You'll make the ice melt, and then the cold barbecued chicken will get warm, and the deviled eggs will go off, and the watermelon will get mushy. And the iced tea will taste like hot tea."

Bug's mouth was watering. "What about dessert?"

"Cupcakes. Frosted red, white, and blue. I'm nothing if not a patriot."

"Can we go now?" Bug asked.

"It's eight forty-five," Mama objected.

Bug didn't care. It was her first beach day of the season! "Please!"

"Let a woman drink her coffee first," Mama said.

"But if we don't get there soon, it'll be full."

"It won't be full," Mama said.

By ten o'clock, they were rolling their wagon of beach stuff to Tower 19. Danny and Mama laid out one big blanket and folded their towels into squares, like pillows. Phillip set up his giant umbrella—the only one in a sea of towels that grew larger as the morning wore on—and unfolded his chair in the shade. He was wearing his beach uniform: a Hawaiian-print shirt and a pair of Bermuda shorts. Frankie wore the Venice Beach T-shirt that Mama had given him and a Dodgers baseball cap he'd gotten from a game he'd gone to with Phillip. Because he hadn't brought a swimsuit, he'd been loaned a pair of Danny's old trunks.

Mama, Bug, and Danny stripped to their bathing suits and Mama rubbed suntan lotion on all of them. *Finally,* Bug thought, breathing in the smell of coconuts, *it's summer.* "Frankie, would you like some suntan lotion?" Mama offered, but Frankie shook his head and crouched in the shade of the umbrella. He didn't even take off his tennis shoes.

"You're not going to take off your shoes?" Bug asked incredulously. Even Phillip went barefoot at the beach.

Frankie scowled.

"Maybe it's different in Ohio, but in California we like to take off clothes on the beach," Bug said.

"Bug," Mama admonished.

"The California sun is pretty strong," Phillip told Bug. "It's not a bad idea for Frankie to play it safe the first day."

"How is the California sun any stronger than the Ohio sun?" Danny asked. "It's not like we're in the tropics."

"Don't be rude, Daniel," Mama said.

"Ha!" Bug said. "That's like telling the ocean not to be wet."

"Shut up, Cockroach!" Danny said. The insult was so old, it was barely an insult anymore.

"You shut up, *Danielle*," Bug said. This insult was brand-new. And it did the trick. The red half-dollars blooming on Danny's cheeks proved this.

"Daniel!" Danny insisted.

"Right." Bug was delighted to have found a crack. "Like I said. *Danielle*."

"Who wants watermelon?" Phillip asked, breaking out a Tupperware.

That shut Bug and Danny up. They sat on the sand, eating, spitting the black seeds into two separate piles. They used to play a game to see who got more seeds, and another game to see how far they could flick the seeds off their thumbnail, but Bug suspected *Daniel* would think this was immature.

The day grew warmer, the crowds flooding the beach like an invading army. Bug wanted to swim, but she needed a buddy if she wanted to go in past her knees. That was Mama's rule.

She looked at Mama, who was lying on her towel, eyes closed, like a lizard absorbing the heat. She knew Mama needed to be "one degree below hell" before she'd get into the cold water. Phillip was a no-go. Danny was in his trunks, playing solitaire on a towel. But no way was she going to ask him! That left Frankie.

"Do you want to swim?" Bug asked.

The face Frankie made was like Bug had offered him their slimy, spit-out watermelon seeds for a snack.

"Doesn't *anyone* want to go for a swim?" Bug moaned.

"Sleeping," Mama said.

Now Bug was mad. It was the first time she'd been to the beach all summer. And they'd been here almost an hour. This wasn't fair. Not at all. She was gearing up to pitch a fit, to wake Mama up and make her go in, cold or not. But before she did, Danny put down his cards. "I'll go."

Part of Bug wanted to say *thanks but no thanks*. That would show Danny that he wasn't the only one who needed space. But

Bug didn't want space. She wanted her brother back. And she really, really wanted to go swimming.

"Fine," she said, trying to make it sound like she didn't care.

But then Danny took off racing toward the water, and Bug ran after him. Neither slowed their pace when they hit the surf's frothy edge, because they both knew if you hesitated even for a moment, you'd chicken out. Even in July, the water was cold!

Shockingly cold for the first moment. Breathtaking. And then, after you'd survived that, after you'd earned it, it was refreshing and perfect.

Bug floated on her back. The sky was blue, the waves were rolling but not crashing. Kip was on duty, and Bug could see him squint at her from the blue platform of the lifeguard tower. She waved. He gave her a thumbs-up, which made Bug feel good. This was still *her* beach.

They swam out to the edge of the breakers, strong swimmers the both of them. As soon as Bug had been old enough, Mama had put all three of them in lessons at the Y. Coming from Visalia, a small city in the middle of the state, she was nervous to suddenly be around all that water and not know what to do in it.

A few surfers were still at it, so Bug and Danny treaded water, staying out of their path. Bug watched them paddle, catch the waves, wondering how it would feel to let the ocean give you a ride like that.

From the shore came the muffled sounds of happy screams, paddleball games, radios. The soundtrack of summer.

Danny popped up next to her and spit water through the gap in his teeth. In pictures of their father, he always had a broad smile, showing off the exact same gap. When she'd gotten her grown-up teeth, Bug hoped she would have the gap. But she didn't.

"Can you see Mom?" That was another change with Danny. Until recently, he'd called her Mama too.

"Right there." Bug pointed to Phillip's umbrella, like a bull's-eye on the beach. Frankie and Phillip were huddled underneath it.

"Guess they're both allergic to water," Danny said.

"Must run in the family," Bug said.

As soon as they got out of the water, Danny became Daniel again, taking his skateboard to the boardwalk. "I'll catch you later," he called to Bug. He was friendly enough about it, but she felt all the betrayal and anger return.

She thought about asking Frankie to play cards, but he'd only say no. So she flopped down on her towel and grabbed her book out of the beach bag. Mama had brought the diary of Anne Frank, which was on Bug's school's summer reading list, but Bug had added her own selection, a book that her friend Beth Ann had loaned her.

Mama pulled her big round sunglasses—her Jackie-O's, Phillip called them—over her nose. "I didn't realize *Flowers in the Attic* was on your summer reading list."

"Whoever put the diary of Anne Frank on a summer reading list either didn't read it or doesn't understand what summer is about," Bug said.

Mama smiled.

"Also, this one is about people hiding in an attic too," Bug added.

Mama laughed and put down her book, which was something by Sidney Sheldon. Her nightstand at home was full of big historical books or biographies of war heroes, but Mama also understood the particulars of a beach read.

"Want to play Crazy Eights?" Mama asked.

It was what Bug always played with Danny. Playing with Mama felt like a sort of defeat. Still, she said okay.

Mama shuffled the cards. "Frankie, do you want to play?"

Frankie shook his head.

"Must be some book that has you so engrossed," Mama said.

"Not a book," Frankie said. "It's the map."

"A map of what?" Mama asked.

"The Midnight Marauder."

Bug jumped up. "Can I see?"

Frankie nodded. Bug abandoned the card game to look over Frankie's shoulder. It was a map of Greater Los Angeles with black dots on it.

"What are the dots for?" Bug asked.

"They are where the attacks were," Frankie explained. "I'm looking for a pattern."

Bug peered closer.

"See here." Frankie traced a trio of dots on the map. "All these were near each other. But then there's this one, in Burbank. It's an outlier."

Bug didn't know what an *outlier* was, but she did know where Burbank was. Beth Ann lived there. She said it was near all the movie studios and that sometimes she saw movie stars when she went to the grocery store, to which Renée, another girl at school who lived in Beverly Hills, had said that *she* saw movie stars just walking down her street. This, they all suspected, was a lie. Everyone knew that famous people didn't just walk down the streets. Not even in Beverly Hills. No one walked here. Danny even had a record with a song that went, "Nobody walks in L.A."

Except for Venice. It was why Mama had settled here. Arriving in Los Angeles with Bug as a baby and Danny four years old, she got off the Greyhound bus and asked someone what was the best place to live in L.A. without a car. The answer was Venice.

So they moved here. And it was true, people walked here. On the boardwalk, on Main Street, on Abbot Kinney, on Speedway. Though you didn't see movie stars in Venice. Well, Danny thought he might have seen Prince once at the record store, but he wasn't positive.

"What does that mean, that it's an outlier?" Bug asked, hoping she got the word right.

Frankie shrugged. "Not sure. Arcadia is kind of in the middle. Just trying to find a pattern. Aside from yellow houses, I read he likes houses near the freeway."

Was that true? The freeway wasn't so near their house, but close enough you could hear the rivery *whoosh* of it at night.

"How close to the freeway have the victims been?" she asked.

Frankie held out the map to show, but then Phillip interrupted. "Beatrice," he said. "Why don't you show Frankie the boardwalk?"

For once, Bug actually didn't want to go to the boardwalk. But Phillip was already pulling out some money. "Here. For ice cream."

"We haven't had lunch yet," Bug reminded him.

He looked at Frankie. "It's a holiday. Live a little."

"This isn't a boardwalk," was the first thing Frankie said.

"What do you mean, it's not a boardwalk?" Bug asked.

"It's cement, not wooden planks. That's what makes something a *board*walk."

"It is too a boardwalk!" Bug said defensively, though as soon as she said it, she realized there were no boards. But still. Who was Frankie to tell her otherwise? This was *her* beach. She knew every part of it. From the punk rockers, hanging out in front of the place that sold pizza for a quarter a slice. To Muscle Beach, where Duane and Randy worked out. To the ice cream stand, where her friend Bian worked.

As if to prove her point, as they walked toward the ice cream stand, Zeus came rolling down the boardwalk, wearing a Speedo bathing suit with the stars and stripes on it, and carrying his boom box.

"Zeus! Zeus!" she called, waving. "That's Zeus," she told Frankie. "He's my friend."

Zeus used his toe stopper to come to a halt right in front of them. Frankie stared with that same puzzled expression he'd been wearing since he arrived.

"We the people signed the paper two hundred eleven years ago today," Zeus said, "which makes it the birthday of the US of A. Go get your skates on, Bugsy, and roll with me."

"He always talks like that," Bug whispered to Frankie. To Zeus she replied, "I wish I could skate with you, but I need new skates. My feet grew two sizes last year."

"Better to grow than to shrink," Zeus said. "If you can't question, can you even think?" He did a twirl and then, peering behind him, began to skate backward. "Bye-bye, Bugsy and Bugsy's friend."

"Frankie," Frankie said.

"Bug and Frankie. Frankie and Bug," Zeus said, skating away.

Bug did not like that she'd been joined with Frankie, and then put *behind* Frankie. This was her boardwalk. These were her friends. Frankie didn't know a thing about it.

They carried on in silence until they reached the ice cream stand. The line snaked past the stand where you could buy a grain of rice with your name inscribed on it.

"Why don't we go over there?" Frankie asked, pointing to the inferior ice cream stand. "The line is shorter."

"Because this place has the best ice cream is why, and because Bian is my friend and . . . ," Bug said, running out of patience with Frankie, who didn't know anything about boardwalks or the best ice cream in Venice and wouldn't even swim. "It's my regular spot."

As the line inched forward, Bug was excited to see Bian. The stand was open only in the summer; during the rest of the year, Bian went to school somewhere not close to the ocean and so Bug never saw her. "This is Frankie," she announced when they got to the front of the line. "He's Phillip's nephew. Here for the summer. This is Bian. She's from Vietnam," Bug started to explain. "She came over on a boat. Not a ship like on *Love Boat* but like a rickety canoe."

Bian smiled politely and looked at the long line. "Nice to meet you. Welcome to Venice."

"I haven't been to the beach this summer because my stupid brother needs space," Bug said, but Bian cut her off.

"Sorry. No time to talk now. You want your usual?"

Deflated, Bug nodded and turned to Frankie. "I always get caramel swirl. Do you want that?"

"I'll get vanilla."

"Really? Just vanilla? That's so boring."

Frankie shrugged. Bug gave Bian two dollars.

Frankie ate his ice cream in slow, circular licks. Bug watched him, feeling itchy with anger. She'd wasted all her conversation time with Bian introducing Frankie. And Frankie didn't even seem impressed about the boat. He'd been sent out here to save her summer, and so far he'd done squat about it. She was about to give him a piece of her mind when she remembered Phillip saying that you "catch more flies with honey." Meaning you were supposed to be sweet instead of sour if you wanted people to do stuff for you. An idea Bug had never had much luck with, but maybe she would now.

She took a deep breath and a giant bite of ice cream and turned to Frankie. "It's really great around here, don't you think?" she began.

Frankie shrugged.

"Like, there's so much stuff to do. You can roller-skate or surf or swim or play on the swings." Bug pointed to a bank of swings in the middle of the sand.

"It's weird here," Frankie said.

Bug knew people thought Venice was weird, and maybe it was, but it was her home. Still, she swallowed her irritation along with her ice cream. She was honey, catching flies.

"I suppose they don't have weird people in Ohio," she mused.

"They have weird people everywhere," he replied.

Now Bug was confused, because he'd just insulted Venice as weird but he was saying Ohio was weird too. She took another deep breath and switched tacks. "So, do you like the beach?"

"It's okay," Frankie said.

"Because if you like the beach, we could come here sometime, together."

"I dunno. I'll be pretty busy this summer."

"Busy? Doing what?"

Frankie scanned the crowded beach, as if looking for something very specific. Then, still staring at the horizon, he told Bug, "I'm going to catch the Midnight Marauder."

*M*uscle Beach

TWO NIGHTS LATER the Midnight Marauder struck again.

"It looks bad," Mama told Phillip the following morning as they drank coffee in Bug's kitchen. Frankie was there too, head stuck in his map.

"It looks bad because it *is* bad," Phillip said, taking the newspaper from Mama.

"Should I stay home?" Mama asked. "Hedvig is visiting her son today."

"You never stay home," Bug said. "Unless Danny or I are sick." But then Bug thought about it. If Mama stayed home, maybe they could go to the beach. "But maybe you should. We might be in grave danger."

"We're not in grave danger," Frankie said. "I already told you. The Midnight Marauder doesn't strike in the day. That's why he's called the Midnight Marauder and not the Noon Marauder."

Bug scowled at Frankie. It was one thing to not want to go to the beach, but another thing to keep her from going. "I still think we'd be safest at the beach," Bug said. "Surrounded by all those people."

Phillip stirred his coffee, his spoon clanking against the mug. "She's not wrong."

Bug grinned in triumph. Until Phillip added, "Alas, I have lessons all day today so I'll be out until dinner."

Mama slurped down her last drops of coffee, and then she went to wake up Danny, who usually slept until past ten. Bug listened to the muffled sounds of an argument—she couldn't make out the specifics, but she guessed it was Danny's version of *not fair*. Mama emerged looking end-of-day tired, even though it was not yet eight o'clock. "Daniel will watch you two today," she announced.

Bug was jubilant. If Danny was watching them, that meant they were going to the beach! Mama and Phillip left for work. Danny went back to sleep. Frankie looked at his map and read the newspaper. He didn't talk to Bug. Even though it was her apartment he was sitting in. Her newspaper she was reading.

Finally, Danny emerged.

"Can we go to the beach now?" Bug asked.

"The beach?" Frankie asked.

"Yeah. That's what we're doing today." She turned to Danny. "Right?"

Danny looked like Mama before her coffee, even though he didn't drink coffee. "Yeah, I'll take you to the beach," he said, and went back into his room to change.

"You should change too," Bug told Frankie.

Frankie frowned. "I don't want to go to the beach."

Bug was about to say *too bad* when she remembered Phillip's rule about flies and honey. "It'll be fun."

"I don't have time to waste at the beach!"

"Wasting time is what the beach is for."

"Then you go. The first twenty-four hours after a crime are the most important for collecting evidence."

"Danny's in charge and he said we're going to the beach, so we're going."

"I don't want to."

"Well, tough. There's two of us and one of you, and if you don't go, I'll tell Phillip on you and he'll tell your parents and you'll get in trouble."

She'd added the last bit just for insurance. She didn't mean to scare Frankie. But she could tell by his expression that she had, and she felt kind of bad. So she added, in a softer voice, "It's fun at the beach. You'll see."

Frankie didn't look too sure about this. But he folded up his map and put it in his backpack.

According to the rules, they were supposed to go directly to Tower 19 and check in with Kip. But as soon as they got to the board-walk, Danny put down his skateboard and took off.

"Where are you going?" Bug asked, jogging to keep up. When Danny didn't answer, she added, "We're supposed to go to Tower Nineteen. Mama said."

Danny rolled his eyes, like Bug was such a baby, listening to what Mama said, still calling her Mama. At last she saw where he was headed. To Muscle Beach. It had once been part of their routine, to come here for an hour or two and watch the guys work out. Bug enjoyed it, but that was back when time on the beach wasn't so precious.

"Danny's taking us to Muscle Beach," Bug told Frankie when he caught up. "It's boring, just a bunch of people exercising on rings and bars and stuff. You don't want to do that, do you?" she asked, hoping Frankie would say no and then it would be two against one and Danny would have to go to Tower 19.

Frankie smirked at her. "Danny's in charge, so we have to do what he says."

Bug's earlobes went hot, but she refused to lose her temper, not with so many people around. So she led Frankie through the chain-link entrance. Muscle Beach looked like a gym—it had parallel bars and uneven bars and rings and barbells—except for the floor, which was sand.

A lot of the regulars were there, Randy with his short-on-top-long-on-bottom haircut, Duane with his glistening Afro, Bill with his faded but still creepy skull tattoos he'd gotten in the army. Bug pointed each person out to Frankie.

"Who's that?" Frankie asked, pointing to the parallel bars.

"That's Vanessa," Bug replied. She was one of a handful of women who worked out here, and she was every bit as strong as the guys.

"I've never seen a girl look like that," Frankie said, watching Vanessa hold herself in a plank, her muscles taut and bulging, her veins as sinewy as ropes.

"Let's go say hi to Duane and Randy," Bug said, pointing to

the area under the rings, where they were standing with Danny and a few other exercisers. None of them were working out. They seemed to be in the midst of a heated conversation. About the Midnight Marauder.

"I told my cousin, we got to be locked and loaded," Randy said. "So we can take him down."

"Yeah. Cops don't do squat," Duane said. "We gotta take care of him ourselves."

"That's why we do what we do," Randy said. "We stay strong. To take on the threat."

"You can't just use strength," Frankie said, stepping into the fray.

They all turned to look at him. Bug waited for them to laugh. Little kids weren't usually welcomed at Muscle Beach.

"Who's this?" Randy asked.

"That's Frankie," Danny said. "Bug's friend."

"He's not my friend!" Bug retorted, but no one paid her any mind.

"You can't catch the Midnight Marauder with just strength," Frankie said, unfazed by Bug's denunciation. "You have to use your brain." He tapped his forehead. "He's a psychopathic killer."

"Psycho killer, like that Talking Heads song?" Randy asked.

Frankie looked stumped. Bug wondered if they had the Talking Heads in Ohio.

"Psychopaths are meticulous planners," Frankie said. "Not impulsive. They have really high IQs. So it's not enough to be strong or have weapons. You have to be smarter than them. To figure out their patterns. To understand them. If we can understand the Midnight Marauder, we can catch him."

"How you do that?" Randy asked.

Here Frankie pulled out his map, and as everyone huddled around him, he explained what the dots meant, how he was looking for patterns. Bug waited for Randy and Duane to laugh, to tell him to take his pretend game and go home. But they all leaned forward, quietly listening as Frankie explained all the things he'd learned.

They were so respectful, as if they didn't think it was silly or babyish for an eleven-year-old to catch a serial killer, Bug tried to imagine how they'd react if *she* were the one investigating the killer. A knot tightened in her stomach, because she knew the answer: they would pat her on the head, call her a cute kid, maybe even laugh at her. Maybe Mama was right. It *was* different for girls.

"Personally," Bill said, "I'd rather just take him out. Like we did in Nam. With brute force."

"Naw, the kid's right," Duane said. "We need the brain and the brawn." He looked at Frankie. "You figure out who he is. Then we'll go take him down."

"Deal," Frankie said, sticking out his hand to shake.

Duane spit in his hand and took Frankie's hand.

None of them so much as looked at Bug.

Finally, Danny left Muscle Beach and took them to Tower 19. They had barely laid out their towels when Danny stood up. Bug, thinking he was ready to go swimming, jumped up too. But Danny started walking, away from the water.

"Where are you going?" Bug asked.

"Muscle Beach."

"But we just got here. And Mama said we were supposed to stay together."

"You have Frankie," he said.

"Frankie won't swim." He hadn't even packed his bathing suit.

"I'll be back in a bit. And watch my board." Danny pointed to his skateboard on the sand.

"Danny," she whined.

"Right back," he repeated.

But he wasn't right back. Bug waded into the ocean up to her knees, staring longingly at the waves. She was at the beach, but she wasn't allowed to swim. This struck her as the height of unfair.

She gave up and went back to the sand. Frankie was surveying the beach using Mama's whale-watching binoculars he'd borrowed for the day.

"You really think the Midnight Marauder is on Venice Beach?" she asked him.

Frankie put down the binoculars and looked at Bug. "He could be anywhere."

An hour later, Danny still was not back. Frankie and Bug ate their lunches and drank their sodas. As was always the case after drinking soda, Bug had to pee. Normally she'd go in the water, but she couldn't if she could only wade in to her knees.

When she felt like she was about to pee her pants, she stood up, defiant. "Come on," she told Frankie, brushing the sand off her legs. "We're leaving."

They packed up and walked to the smelly public restrooms. A homeless guy with matted hair was napping with his German shepherd by the drinking fountains. "Do you have to go?" Bug asked. "The boys' room is around the other side."

Frankie had drunk just as much soda as Bug and seemed to be doing a bathroom dance of his own. He looked around a moment, then shook his head. "No. I'm okay."

Bug's stream of pee went so long she could count slowly to twenty while she was going. When she was done, they went back to Muscle Beach. The fog was rolling in off the ocean. It would soon be too cold to swim even if Danny did come with. And Danny didn't seem to be in any hurry. Bug found him in the middle of a set of sit-ups, with Duane pinning down his feet.

"You're a big dumb liar," Bug shouted through the chain-link fence. "And we're going home!" Then she dropped his skateboard in the sand, kicking it before marching off toward the boardwalk. "Come on," she called to Frankie, ducking down one of the pedestrian streets that led to Speedway, hoping to ditch Danny. Maybe she'd slip into one of the alleys and lose him for good. The only problem was Mama said Bug was not allowed to be in the alleys because cars sped through them like it was the freeway and she was worried Bug would get hit.

Maybe she would get hit by a car and then Danny would get in trouble. That would show him!

Only Bug didn't want to get hit by a car. And anyway, Danny had nearly caught up, wheezing, "Bug, slow down."

Bug didn't slow down. She sped up, making the light at Pacific, while Danny got stuck at the red. Frankie, who could've waited for Danny, walked briskly to keep up with Bug. Which made her dislike him a teensy bit less.

They turned left on Pacific, the carnival-like atmosphere of the boardwalk giving way to a more sedate stretch of stucco apartment buildings, palm trees, a battalion of VW surfer vans parked on the streets where it didn't cost anything. Bug glanced behind her. Danny had stopped skating and was bent over his knees.

"Maybe we should wait," Frankie said. "He looks hurt."

"It would serve him right!" One day he'd taken her to the beach—*one* day—and they didn't even get to go swimming. She felt like crying.

Bug could see the school playground on her corner in the distance. The punks were hanging out there. She saw their bright-colored hair, their spiky Mohawks. Frankie saw them too, mouth agape.

"Those are the good punks," Bug told him. "They're nice."

"Are there bad punks?" Frankie asked.

"The skinheads," Bug replied. "They beat people up just for fun."

Danny caught up, breath ragged. "Why are you being such a brat?" he gasped at Bug.

"*I'm* the brat?" Bug roared. "First you ditch me this whole summer, and then on the one day you're supposed to take me to the beach, you ditch me again."

"I wasn't ditching you," he said. "I was trying to take care of you."

"Ha!" Bug scoffed. "You have a funny way of showing it."

"Look, I'm sorry. Let's go to Dixon's. I'll buy you Bomb Pops."

Bug didn't want Danny to get off that easy, but an ice pop sounded good, and staying mad took up so much energy, and she'd been so busy being mad at Frankie she was kind of worn out. "Fine."

They turned off Pacific Avenue and walked up Westminster. Before they got to the Hermit House, Danny turned to Bug. "Do you want to cross the street?"

Bug could tell Danny was trying to be nice, to make it up to her. Because normally he made fun of her for being scared to walk in front of the Hermit House. The place was huge, as big as Bug's entire building, only it belonged to one person: the Hermit. He almost never came out, but she'd seen him

peering out of the window by the alley, long-haired, dead-eyed. A bogeyman catty-corner across the street. Bug got a chill every time she passed by, which Danny said was because the overgrown trees blocked the sun, but Bug knew better. There was evil inside that house.

Not that Bug was going to admit it, not after she'd been trying so hard to prove her grown-up-ness. "I'm okay," she said.

They carried on down the block. The fog rolling in off the ocean hadn't made it inland yet, so it was still warm over here, but Bug felt it again—the icy coldness—when she stepped onto the section of the sidewalk in front of the Hermit House.

Bug thought of what Frankie had said about the Midnight Marauder. *He could be anywhere.*

She shivered and hurried past.

Skinheads

ON SATURDAY MORNINGS, Bug, Danny, and Mama went out to eat at the Chinese Diner. That wasn't the restaurant's real name, but everyone called it that because it served Chinese food and all-day breakfasts. And Mama said it was the best deal in town. "An omelet, home fries, toast, and coffee for two bucks. Can't beat that."

Mama slept later than normal that Saturday because she'd had to work late again, so it was closer to lunchtime when they set off. Mama was silent and grumpy because they were out of coffee, and she always said she was no good until she'd seen the bottom of her first cup.

As they walked up Westminster toward Abbot Kinney, Bug

dragged a stick along the chain-link fence by the school, enjoying the *rat-tat-tat* sound it made, in a nice kind of concert with the *thwack, thwack* of Danny's skateboard hitting the grooves in the sidewalk. So she didn't see them until it was too late.

There, right on the corner. Skinheads.

Everything about them glinted: the zippers on their boots, the patches on their leather jackets, the severe lines of their always-fresh buzz cuts, and scariest of all, the sharp things Bug couldn't see but heard they kept inside their jackets.

There were lots of gangs around Venice, but the skinheads were different. Mama said if you weren't bothering the other gangs, they wouldn't bother you. But the skinheads . . . bothering people was what they did.

Bug counted five of them. Two of them looked pretty young, around Danny's age, but the rest looked like grown-ups. She'd seen skinheads before, near the skate park in the Marina and at the old abandoned lifeguard tower that was their unofficial hangout. But this was the first time she'd seen them so close to home.

Bug tightened her grip on the stick. "Mama," she whispered, gesturing toward the skinheads. "Let's go home. I'm not hungry anymore."

Mama was wearing her Jackie-O sunglasses, so it was impossible to see her eyes. But Bug knew by the way her mother squared her shoulders and stared straight ahead that she'd seen the skinheads and had no intention of changing course. Mama was not scared of anything. Apparently, that was why Bug's father had fallen in love with her. At least that was what Danny said.

"Mama," Bug whined.

Mama didn't answer but reached for Bug's hand, forcing her to drop the stick. Danny was on her other side, now holding his board; Mama didn't take his hand.

The light at Abbot Kinney turned red right as they got to the corner. Suspense churned in Bug's stomach, like when she watched *Poltergeist*. They had to cross Abbot Kinney and go two more blocks to the right. They could cross Westminster now and wait for the light to change on the other side of the street. Or jaywalk across the road.

But Mama didn't do any of that. She waited on the corner, with the skinheads a few feet away, holding really still in a way that made Bug stop fidgeting too.

"Hey, nice deck," one of the skinheads called to Danny, and Bug thought maybe it would be okay if they were complimenting Danny's skateboard, until he added, "Who'd you steal it from?"

Danny's shoulders stiffened.

"Maybe he snuck it across the border," another said. "Didn't know Mexican monkeys could skate." Then he called Danny an even meaner name that made the hair on Bug's neck rise.

"I'm Salvadoran, not Mexican," Danny proclaimed.

This was another change in Danny. Since Bug moved out of their room, he'd decorated it with Salvadoran flags and begun declaring to everyone he was from El Salvador. He'd started taking Spanish lessons every Monday from a Salvadoran teacher in the Pico-Union area near downtown and asking Mama to learn to cook things like *carne guisada*, which Mama said she would, if she ever learned to cook. He had also started pestering Mama about a trip to El Salvador to meet all the aunts and uncles who lived there, which Mama said they could do but not until the war there ended. Bug was mildly perplexed about his sudden interest in their father's homeland, but right now, she just wanted him to shut up about it.

"Mexico. El Lamador. What's the diff?" one skinhead asked.

Danny started to answer, but Bug kicked him. "Cut it out," she hissed.

This was a mistake, because the skinheads were now looking at her. And at Mama. "Oh, is that your mommy?" one of the skinheads asked Danny.

"That's one hot mama," said another.

"Seems like she has a taste for the dark meat," the oldest one said. "At least with *one* of the kids. You like to get around, hot mama?"

It wasn't the first time people thought Bug and Danny had different fathers. In addition to the gap between his teeth, Danny had inherited their father's wiry brown hair and his coffee-colored skin, which got very dark in summer. Bug looked more like Mama, with green eyes and only slightly darker skin that made people ask her if she was Italian. But it was the first time Bug was relieved by the mistake. And the relief was followed by a surge of shame.

"You like to share the love, hot mama," one said, making a rude gesture between his legs. "Spread it around. You should give me a go."

The other skinheads laughed until Mama turned and ever so slightly lowered her glasses. Her expression, a little amused, a little disgusted, was exactly how she looked at Bug and Danny when they had fart contests. It was a look that let you know she was not—remotely—impressed.

The light changed. Mama and Danny and Bug started into the crosswalk, the skinheads following right behind them. Bug could hear the heavy thud of their boots. Every cell in her body wanted to speed up, but Mama kept walking at her slow, steady pace.

After what felt like hours, they reached the other side of the intersection. Bug wondered what would happen now. Would the skinheads follow them to the diner? A few weeks ago they'd beat up a tourist from Japan inside a store in the middle of the day! Bug had heard about it on the evening news.

At the next block, the skinheads turned left toward Lincoln. Bug, Danny, and Mama carried on in silence until they reached the Chinese Diner. Only when they were sitting in their booth did Bug's legs start knocking together. Mama put a hand on Bug's knee.

"It's okay," Mama said. "We're okay."

But it didn't feel okay. It felt like the opposite of okay.

The waitress came by to take their orders, a formality because they always got the same thing. "The usual?" she asked.

Danny and Mama said yes, but a whirlwind of feelings—relief and shame and fear and anger—spun in Bug's chest, making it hard to speak.

"For all three of us," Mama told the waitress. She turned to Bug. "Would you like a hot chocolate, too?"

Normally Bug loved the hot chocolate here, made with a

powder that collected into a delicious paste at the bottom of the mug and topped with flounces of whipped cream. But at the moment, not even hot chocolate could calm her. The whirlwind had become a tornado, and after the waitress left, all of Bug's mixed-up feelings came bursting out.

"Why did you say that thing about being Salvadoran, not Mexican?" she shouted at Danny.

"Because I am," Danny replied in a voice as quiet as Bug's was shrill. "We are."

"And why didn't you do anything?" she yelled at Mama.

Mama gripped the empty coffee mug. "They're bullies, trying to scare us, Bug. I wasn't about to give them that victory." The busboy came by to fill Mama's mug. Mama nodded her thanks and took a long slurp before turning back to Bug. "If we'd crossed the street, they would've won. If we went fast, they would've won."

"So what?"

"Then the next time they saw us, they would've come after us twice as hard," Danny said.

She didn't understand what this meant. And worse, the way he said it, so seriously, in a voice that had once sounded so much like Bug's that people always mistook them on the phone but now was a man's voice, made Bug feel more left out than ever. She and

Danny had always been the team. But now it felt like Danny and Mama were the team.

"*I hate you!*" she cried at Danny. The words flew out, followed by a spate of hot tears because she loved Danny. But she hated him too. Which was confusing. Like being relieved and ashamed that the skinheads hadn't realized she was Salvadoran was confusing.

Danny didn't look hurt or angry so much as surprised, which made Bug want to cry even more. "Why do you hate me?" he asked.

"You ruined everything!" Bug sniffed. "You wrecked the whole summer. I can't go to the beach because of you, and I'm stuck with Frankie!"

"That wasn't Daniel," Mama said. "That was me. If you need to hate someone, hate me."

"I hate both of you!" Bug shouted. "And Phillip."

"What's Phillip got to do with it?" Danny asked.

"I don't know," Bug said. She'd never said she hated Phillip before, and it made her feel just terrible. "I hate those skinheads the most."

"Well," Danny said, "at least they deserve it."

Mama sighed and drank more coffee. "No one deserves it."

"How can you say that?" Bug asked. "After what they said. To us. To you. And they beat up that tourist kid for no good reason. You should hate them."

"Well, I don't," Mama replied. "I feel sorry for them."

The things they'd said to Danny. The creepy way they'd looked at Mama, like they were yard dogs and she was a piece of meat. And *she* felt sorry for *them*? Sometimes Bug did not understand Mama at all.

"I know they seem tough, but people who need to exert force to make themselves feel strong are weak. They're scared people who need to scare people." Mama shook her head and frowned. "It's pretty pathetic when you think about it. That they need to pick on a teenage boy, a woman, and a little girl."

"I'm not a little girl," Bug said, wiping the tears and snot from her face with a paper napkin.

"Of course you're not," Mama said, handing Bug another napkin.

"And I'm not just a teenage boy," Danny added. "I'm the man of the family."

"Are you?" Mama sounded amused.

"Dad's gone. So yeah, I am."

"I suppose you are," Mama said, putting her hand atop Danny's.

"I'm sorry you hate me, Bug," Danny said in a quiet voice.

Bug started to cry again, great gusty sobs that she could neither control nor understand. She wanted to tell Danny that she didn't really hate him. She missed him. And she was mad at him. She was jealous that he looked like their father. And also relieved that she did not. She didn't want him to be the man of the family, but to go back to being the big brother of the family. She wanted to say so many things she didn't have the words for.

Their waitress returned with their meals and took one look at them, Bug crying, now Mama crying a little too. "You don't want the food? I can take it back."

No one answered at first, and then Mama started to laugh, accepting the platter of pancakes, along with her eggs and Danny's lo mein. Then Danny started to laugh too, and even though Bug didn't much feel like laughing, it was contagious when the two of them went off, so she was joining them, even though nothing felt funny at the moment.

hivery

DANNY DIDN'T TELL BUG that he was working out at Muscle Beach every day now, but she knew. He'd gotten a sweatband like Duane's and a canteen for water that he filled up in the sink before he set out. He didn't tell Bug not to tell Mama what he was doing, but she knew that, too.

She desperately wanted to ask him why he was working out: Was it because of the Midnight Marauder? Because of the skinheads? Because he was Daniel, the man of the family? All of the above?

Not so long ago, she could ask her brother everything: *How fast do clouds move? Where do wolves live? Is Boy George a boy or a girl?* And *What was our father like?*

From Mama, Bug knew that her father, also called Daniel,

was from a part of El Salvador called Antiguo Cuscatlán, near the capital of San Salvador, where he'd been a university professor and a leader in the teachers' union, until that had gotten him in trouble with the government and he had to leave home or get put in jail. He'd moved to California and had gotten involved with a group that was fighting for farmworker rights. Mama was also part of the group, and that was how they met.

Mama said Bug's father was warm and funny and dedicated to making the world a better place. She also said he was the smartest person she'd ever met. He spoke three languages: English, Spanish, and Nahuatl, which sounded to Bug like a made-up language but Mama said was the language of the mighty Aztecs, from which their father, and also Bug and Danny, were descended.

Bug had studied the Aztecs in third grade and knew they once had an ancient empire with pyramids like the Egyptians and a complicated calendar based on the sun—the class had made sun stones for their year-end project. Sometimes her father also felt like something she had learned about in a class.

They had only one photo album of him, the pictures glued and reglued into place after repeated thumbing. There were lots of snapshots of her father and Mama—some of them out protesting in the fields, another of them getting married at city hall, and of course a bunch with little Danny. But there was just one picture with Bug in it. And she wasn't really in it. The picture was of her father holding Danny with one arm, touching Mama's pregnant stomach with the other. According to Mama, he used to talk to her belly. "Hello, Bug," he would call. And that was why even though Mama had named her Beatrice, she only ever called her Bug.

The last photo in the album was taken the day Bug was born. There was Mama holding her in a bundle of blankets, Danny grasping Bug's tiny hand, and Aunt Teri hovering in the corner. But not her father. He had died in a car accident seven weeks earlier. This was a kind of unfair that hurt too much to speak of.

Talking about their father made Mama sad, even ten years after he'd died. So this was why Bug relied on Danny for stories. According to Danny, their father played harmonica and sang and was obsessed with playing soccer, which he called football, and he could fall asleep anywhere and doodled, constantly, while he worked. He couldn't grow a beard no matter how hard he tried, but once for a little while he did grow a mustache that Mama teased him about. He thought iodine cured all ailments and carried a bottle around in his pocket and made Danny gargle with it to get rid of sore throats.

Bug could hardly remember being four, and she was only six

years away from that age, so she never could understand how Danny remembered all this. Still, she clung to these details, as well as Danny's memories of their grandparents—Mama's parents—who he also remembered. He said Bug had met them, only she didn't remember because they'd moved to Venice on that Greyhound when she was just a few months old. Danny remembered that, too. He said Mama cried the whole way down. Mama almost never cried, so Bug found this hard to believe, but she knew Danny wouldn't lie about such a thing.

And even if she didn't believe Danny, there was no one else she could ask. Certainly not Mama. If she got sad when Bug asked about her father, she went blank when Bug asked about her grandparents, or why they never visited them, even though Visalia was only five hours away. Danny and Bug used to scheme about sneaking up to visit their grandparents together, without Mama knowing. But the last time Bug brought this up to Danny, he just frowned and said he didn't want to. This was another way *Daniel* had changed on her.

Now Bug watched Danny dress for Muscle Beach each morning, hoping she would be invited to go with, but she wasn't. With each passing week, his muscles seemed to grow, along with the distance between them.

And so the precious summer dribbled away. Bug stayed with Hedvig, or wandered around the playground, bored and lonely. When Phillip wasn't working, he took Frankie out. And when he was working, Frankie stayed upstairs. Bug could hear him padding around. But she did not invite him to play with her, and he didn't invite her to play with him.

"Did something happen with you two?" Mama asked Bug one night.

"No."

"Why aren't you playing together?"

"Frankie's weird," Bug replied.

Mama pursed her lips into a disappointed frown. "The day I meet someone not weird is the day I go running for the hills."

"What's that mean?"

"It means people are complicated, and everyone is weird in their way."

"Not everyone is weird," Bug said. "Aunt Teri isn't weird."

Mama scoffed at that. "You know who people always say aren't weird? Serial killers. After they're caught, neighbors always says, 'Oh, they seemed so normal.' So maybe normal is weirdest of all."

"Whatever. I just don't want to play with Frankie, okay?"

The truth of the matter was, *Frankie* didn't want to play with

Bug. Here he was, brought in because the real Danny didn't want her anymore. And now the replacement Danny didn't want her either.

One afternoon Bug was at Hedvig's when *As the World Turns* came on. It was the one o'clock soap opera, between *All My Children* at noon and *General Hospital* at two.

"I think that Lily and Holden, it happen for them today," Hedvig said. Lily and Holden were in love but couldn't be together because Lily's mother was rich and Holden was a stable boy.

"Not if Lucinda Walsh has anything to say about it," Bug replied. Lucinda was Lily's mother. She pretty much ran Oakdale.

Hedvig nodded. "You're right. Lucinda will fight. But true love wins." She set down the same tin of cookies she'd had for as long as Bug could remember. Bug grabbed a butter cookie with a petrified cherry in the middle, and right as she was about to bite into it, she saw herself: in Hedvig's apartment, becoming an expert on soap operas, about to eat a snack from Hedvig's pantry of doom.

"I gotta get out of here," she muttered.

"What was that?" Hedvig asked.

She jumped up. "I just remembered something. I've gotta go."

"But they might kiss!" Hedvig protested. "We've waited so long."

Another reason to get away. Kissing, as far as Bug was concerned, was gross, and the soap operas had far too much of it for her liking. "You can tell me what happens later."

She raced outside and hurried toward the tetherball courts. Halfway down the block, she bumped into Frankie.

"Oh, hi," Bug said.

"Hi," Frankie said.

They stared at each other for a second. Bug was about to step past him when she noticed the composition book in his hand. "What's that?"

Frankie kicked at the sidewalk groove with his tennis shoe. The rubber over the toe was half on, half off, like he'd picked at it. "My Midnight Marauder notebook."

"What's in it?"

"Clues."

"Can I see?"

"Sure."

They went to the empty schoolyard and sat at one of the picnic tables next to the shuttered cafeteria. Frankie flipped through the pages. They had maps and news clippings and outlines of patterns and similarities between the attacks. "It's hard because L.A. is so big," he said.

Bug nodded. "Bigger than Delaware and Rhode Island combined." She'd learned that in geography. "But that makes it less likely that we'll get attacked, right?"

"I guess. But it's harder to see a pattern."

"Oh," Bug said.

"A police officer on the news said that people should be on the lookout for any suspicious activity," Frankie said. "So that's what I'm doing." He pointed to a page labeled *Suspects*. It was empty. "There's nothing all that suspicious around here. There are lots of strange people, but that's not the same as evil."

Evil. Bug felt the chill of the Hermit House.

"What about the Hermit?" Bug asked.

"The Hermit?"

"He lives over there." Bug pointed. "In that super-creepy house. He's been there forever and hardly ever comes out."

Frankie looked at her. He had his Dodgers cap pulled low so she couldn't see his eyes, couldn't guess what he was thinking. Probably he thought the same as Danny, that she was a scaredy-cat baby.

"Never mind," Bug said. "I'm sure everybody thinks the killer lives in the creepy house on their street."

Frankie looked up from under his cap and Bug could see his eyes now, bright with curiosity. "No. It's always the quiet neighbor on the block who the neighbors never suspect."

That was kind of what Mama had said. "So . . . so you think it *could* be the Hermit?"

Frankie tugged on the rim of his cap. "I think we should investigate. You want to show me?"

"Sure."

Bug led Frankie to the Hermit House, stopping in front of the bungalow next door, painted turquoise and yellow, with surfboards on the porch. This was usually as far as Bug would go on her own, but with Frankie by her side, she felt braver. "It's right there, and as soon as I step in front, I feel a chill." She shuddered just talking about it. "Danny says it's because the trees are overgrown, but I'm not so sure."

They stared at the Hermit House. Three stories, painted a white that had long ago turned gray. It looked like the Haunted Mansion at Disneyland, only the ghosts here felt real.

Gingerly, Frankie and Bug stepped onto the first square of the Hermit's sidewalk. "It feels cold, right?" Bug asked. "It does to me, anyhow."

"No. You're right. It does feel cold. And not from the trees. It's a shivery cold."

"Exactly. *Shivery*." What a perfect way to describe it. Like the chill you'd sometimes get up your spine. Aunt Teri said those chills meant a spirit was passing by you. Maybe that was it. All the spirits of the people the Hermit had killed were still in the house.

Mama said Aunt Teri was silly and superstitious, but she had also told Bug that bad feelings were her Gut Voice's way of warning her. It seemed like Mama and Teri were both saying the Hermit House was a bad place. And now Frankie thought so too.

Bug was cold, as she always was outside the Hermit House. But it was strange, too, because at that moment, with Frankie by her side, on her team, Bug felt like it had finally become summer.

Leads

FRANKIE AND BUG STARTED a new page in the investigation notebook with the heading *Leads*. In it, they listed all the things they knew about the Hermit.

He did not leave his house. By day, anyway. Frankie had pointed out that just because Bug had never seen him ever leave during the day didn't mean he might not be sneaking out at night. *Like the Midnight Marauder.*

He never opened the shutters over the front windows. Bug and Frankie concluded this because the shutters were overgrown with vines.

He didn't use his front door. This was Frankie's discovery. He'd noticed the leaves and takeout menus and ads for discount car washes, all moldering on the porch. Which suggested that no one ever came or went by the front door.

But maybe he used his side door. It let out onto the alley that ran between San Juan and Westminster. Bug rarely went over there, because she avoided anything in the Hermit House vicinity and because she was not allowed to play in the alleys.

He might have a car. Frankie had discovered a Chevy Malibu, old and rusty but with current registration tags, parked near his side door. Police said the Midnight Marauder stole the cars he used to drive to the attacks, but Bug pointed out that he might have to drive somewhere to steal a car. Frankie said he could take the bus, but Bug said that no one in L.A. took the bus if they could help it.

Bug had been half kidding about the Hermit being the Midnight Marauder, but when she looked at the outline in Frankie's block lettering, taking up two pages, she really did start to wonder if she and Frankie might be onto something. Bug imagined the two of them on the news. Their neighbors would be so impressed with their detective work. "We had no idea," they'd tell Tad Draper, who was Mama's favorite reporter. "Thank goodness those smart kids figured it out."

•••

One afternoon Danny came home, sweaty from his workout. Phillip was teaching, so Bug and Frankie were upstairs in his apartment, working on the investigation book.

Danny poked his head in. "You guys wanna go to the beach?"

"With you?" Bug asked.

"No, with Bono," Danny said. "I'm gonna go shower. If you wanna go, be ready in five."

"More like twenty," Bug muttered. Danny's showers were endless these days, using all the hot water. Still, she wasn't going to begrudge him now that he was being nice.

"I'll get my bathing suit." Bug hopped up. She looked at Frankie, who hadn't budged. "Come on!"

He shook his head. "I'm not going."

"Why not?"

Frankie shrugged.

"It's okay if you don't know how to swim," Bug said generously. "We can splash in the shallow water."

"I know how to swim," Frankie said defensively.

"Are you scared of the waves?" This Bug understood. She'd been munched by them enough. "I can show you how to dive into them. It's only scary at first, and it's okay if you need to hold your nose."

"I'm not scared of the waves." The tip of Frankie's nose went Rudolph-red. "I just don't want to go swimming."

"But I do!" Bug said.

"So go without me," Frankie said without looking at her. Part of her wanted to say, *Fine, I will.* Except another part of her understood how left out he would feel if she did.

They worked in silence until Danny returned, wet from the shower and holding a string bag full of snacks. "You two ready?"

Bug looked at Frankie, sitting on the rug, and knew she could not go without him. Rule number four—always stay together—no longer applied to her and Danny. Now it applied to her and Frankie. She wasn't happy about it. She wanted to go to the beach. But not enough to break the rule.

She sighed heavily. "We're gonna stay here."

She waited for Danny to argue, to cajole her. But he just shrugged and said, "Suit yourself."

She waited for Frankie to say thank you, to acknowledge her sacrifice. But he didn't say anything either, just kept working on the book.

Bug was annoyed. But then they got back to work. After a while, she forgot all about the beach.

he Alley

THE MIDNIGHT MARAUDER struck again. Mama had to work late, and both she and Phillip decided Frankie and Bug should stay with a grown-up, and no amount of Frankie's insistence that they'd be fine during the day helped. So now they were both stuck with Hedvig.

The attack had been in Glendale. Frankie showed it to Bug on a map. It seemed far enough away. To Bug, anyway.

"My son lives in Glendale!" Hedvig cried. "He lives in the hills. Very far from everything. Like sitting pigeons."

"Ducks," Bug corrected.

"That's good," Frankie told Hedvig. "The Midnight Marauder only attacks people in yellow houses near the freeway."

Bug waited for Hedvig to challenge them or say that was nonsense, but just like Duane and Randy, she trusted Frankie's authority. "Really?" she asked.

"That's the pattern," Frankie said.

"How do you know? Does the mayor tell you?" she asked Bug, as if Bug, not Mama, was the one who worked in the press office.

"We're investigating ourselves," Frankie said.

Bug gave Frankie a sneaky kick. They'd agreed not to tell anyone—especially the grown-ups—what they were doing. If it got back to Mama, that would be the end of the investigation.

"What have you found?" Hedvig asked Frankie.

"Lots of things. We have a book, upstairs."

Hedvig didn't look amused, or like she thought they were stupid. She looked interested, maybe even relieved.

"If we were allowed out today, we could investigate more," Bug ventured.

Hedvig didn't even hesitate. "Go!" she said. "Go catch this madman."

Outside, they examined the Hermit House. So far, the most promising lead was the car. If they could prove that the Hermit was driving anywhere on days there were attacks, they'd have real evidence.

"If the miles on the odometer go up after an attack, that's our proof," Bug explained.

"That's really smart," Frankie said.

"Thank you," Bug replied, the compliment sending a delicious warmth up her spine. "But you'll have to check the odometer by yourself, because I'm not allowed in the alley."

"That's okay," Frankie replied.

"Aren't you scared?"

Bug expected Frankie to say no, that he wasn't scared of anything, and all the stuff other boys always bragged about to show how brave they were. But when Frankie replied, "Of course I'm scared," Bug decided he really was brave. Not only was he willing to investigate a potential serial killer living across the way, he'd come all the way from Ohio, by himself, to stay with an uncle he'd never met for the whole summer. Bug could hardly imagine going to stay with Aunt Teri for a week, let alone two months, and she'd known Aunt Teri all her life.

"We can't make it obvious," Bug said. "It has to seem like you're in the alley for a reason."

"I could ride a bike," he said.

"My bike got stolen," Bug said. She looked at Frankie's feet, much smaller than hers, and snapped her fingers. "Roller-skating! The older kids skate in the alley all the time, even though it's kind of bumpy."

"I don't know how to skate," Frankie said.

"Oh." Bug deflated.

"So you'll have to show me," he added.

They ran back into their apartment building to fetch the skates.

"You're back already?" Hedvig asked, sticking her head out of the hallway in front of her apartment.

"Just getting some surveillance tools," Bug said as they bounded up the stairs to her apartment. She dug out her old tennis-shoe skates from the back of Danny's closet, where she still kept her stuff because her room didn't have a proper closet, only a dresser and a bar to hang things on. The skates were too big for Frankie, so Bug stuffed some tissues in the toe box.

At first Frankie was very wobbly, even when holding on to fences and trees. Skate-skate-grab. Skate-skate-grab. All afternoon. By the end of the day, though, Frankie said he was ready for the alley.

The next morning, as soon as Phillip and Mama had both left for work, Bug and Frankie checked in with Hedvig and told her they had investigating to do. "What are you waiting for?" she asked, shooing them outside.

"I'll wait here at the end of the alley," Bug said, making sure to situate herself as far away from the Hermit's property line as possible. "I have the book, so anything you see, skate to me and I'll write it down."

"Got it." Frankie looked nervous. Bug couldn't tell if it was because of the skating or the proximity to the Hermit House, but her own stomach was in snakes.

Frankie took off down the alley. He shuffled more than skated, his hands flailing at his sides. He got about halfway to where the Hermit's car was parked and turned around and shuffle-skated back to Bug.

"Are you okay?" she asked.

He nodded. Perspiration beaded his forehead. "Just getting steady."

"Okay. Want to take a break?"

He shook his head. "Gonna try to go faster this time."

"Okay," Bug said.

As Frankie set off again, Bug felt itchy and anxious, stuck here on the sidewalk, watching his glacial progress. She could walk on her hands faster than he was skating.

But then he began to pick up speed. Instead of shuffling, he was, if not quite gliding, then doing something that looked like skating.

It was at that exact moment that Bug remembered the pothole. Round and deep. Mama had once lost a hubcap driving over it too fast.

She didn't want to yell so close to the Hermit House, so she started fast-walking down the alley, calling Frankie's name. But it was too late. She saw the bright yellow toe stopper dip into the pothole and then Frankie tumbled over, limbs and skates flying out in every direction.

"Oh no!" Bug cried, running to him. He'd propped himself up and was gulping for air as he stared at his knee. It was gross, all pulpy and bloody, with bits of rocks mashed into it.

"Oh, Frankie, you're hurt. Bad."

Frankie wasn't crying. He should've been but wasn't. "I'm okay," he said quietly.

"You're not okay!" Bug wailed. "Should I call an ambulance?"

"I think a first aid kit will do," Frankie said. "And maybe some help, you know, getting up."

"Oh, right." Bug wiped her tears against the sleeve of her shirt and leaned over to help Frankie to his feet. Still on the skates, he slid out from under her. "Maybe we should take these off first," she said.

Bug unlaced the skates—now streaked with blood—and pulled them off. Then she hoisted Frankie up, and together, they limped out of the alley and across the street.

Back home, Bug offered to fix him up. She was feeling steadier now, ashamed for having cried, but Frankie said they ought to ask Hedvig.

"But she might tell!" Bug said.

Frankie shrugged.

Inside, *Ryan's Hope* was playing. Bug expected Hedvig to make a fuss when she saw Frankie's knee, but she surprised her for the second time in two days. "Come to the bathroom," she said. She didn't even make them wait for the commercial.

Sitting Frankie on the toilet, Hedvig used tweezers to remove the pebbles. Bug watched, a wavy, throw-uppy feeling in her stomach (because it had to hurt, and also she was worried about whether those tweezers had ever been cleaned). Frankie just sat there, stoic. Even when Hedvig finished up and dabbed his whole knee with rubbing alcohol. Rubbing alcohol stung so bad! Mama only ever used hydrogen peroxide. But Frankie hardly flinched. Bug decided Frankie might be the bravest person she knew.

When Phillip came home, Hedvig told him Frankie had fallen while learning to roller-skate, which was true even if it wasn't the whole truth. Then she'd looked at Frankie and Bug and winked, as if to say, *Your secret is safe with me.*

And so the investigation continued.

The Stakeout

"I'M SO GLAD YOU AND FRANKIE have become friends," Mama said a few mornings later as she got ready for work. She was drinking coffee. Bug was eating Lucky Charms. Danny was sleeping.

"Yep," Bug said. She was too, but she didn't want Mama to think this got her off the hook for almost wrecking the summer. Besides, now that she and Frankie were hanging out, and now that Mama and Phillip had relaxed the adult-supervision rule, she planned to angle for beach privileges soon, if, that was, she could ever get Frankie to agree to go into the water.

"Have you two talked about anything interesting?" Mama asked.

"Like what?" Bug tried to sound casual as she stirred the sugary gray cereal milk.

"I don't know . . ." Mama trailed off. "Life, I guess."

Bug stole a look at Mama. Did she know? Had someone told her? If she did know, why hadn't she shut down the investigation? It was still going strong, though Bug and Frankie had decided to change strategies, by staking out the front of the Hermit House from the other side—the safe side—of the street.

Mama didn't say anything. She had a way of using silence as invitation to talk, and that was when Bug often got herself into trouble. The trick was to say something without giving anything away. "We just talk about kid stuff," Bug said noncommittally.

Mama finished her coffee, rinsed the cup in the sink, and put it on the drying rack. "Well, if you need to talk to me about anything, let me know, okay?"

"Okay," Bug agreed.

"What are you doing today?"

"We're having a lemonade stand."

"Fun." Mama poked her head into the freezer. "There's two cans of mix in here. Will that be enough?"

"I think so."

"If not, there's some change in the desk drawer. You can buy more at Dixon's." She closed the freezer and kissed Bug on the forehead. "Thanks for making lemonade out of this summer's lemons."

She could hear the apology in Mama's voice. She nodded solemnly. She didn't tell Mama that though this summer was strange and not what she'd expected, it wasn't bad.

After Mama left for work, Bug took the cans of lemonade concentrate and the plastic jug to Phillip's apartment.

"We're having breakfast," Frankie said, opening the door.

"Beatrice," Phillip called. "Would you like some French toast?"

Bug smelled the cinnamon and the eggs, saw the fruit compote Phillip made to put on top. She'd eaten three bowls of cereal, but she would never turn down Phillip's cooking. "Sure." The cans were already growing squishy in her hands. "Can I put these in your freezer?"

Phillip eyed the cans. "What are those for?"

Bug looked at Frankie. "We're having a lemonade stand," he told his uncle.

Phillip arched his eyebrows. "Using concentrate?"

"It's good," Bug said. "It has pulp, even."

Phillip made a face. "You two sit down and eat breakfast, and before I leave for work, I will show you how to make proper lemonade."

Proper lemonade, it turned out, required lemons. Lots of them. Luckily, they grew on trees all over their block, and while Frankie and Bug ate breakfast, Phillip asked a neighbor if he could pick some and came back with a bag full. He sliced them open—the air went sharp with a citrus zing—and plugged in an electric juicer.

He squeezed a few lemons and then handed off the job, explaining, "One cup juice, one cup sugar, four cups water. That's how you make proper lemonade."

Frankie and Bug juiced the remaining lemons. It was pretty fun, the way the juicer made Bug's whole arm vibrate, the way it caught the seeds in the little strainer. After they'd done all the lemons, they mixed the sugar in warm water so it dissolved, then added lemon juice and cold water. Phillip had them taste with a spoon. Sweet and tart and delicious.

Bug reached for the plastic jug.

"No, no, no," Phillip said. "We are a class operation." He went into his china cabinet and pulled out a crystal pitcher. "It's all about the presentation."

Bug and Frankie carried the lemonade to the street, along with a small table, a cooler full of ice, and a tower of plastic cups. Before Phillip left for work, he cut them sprigs of mint from the herb garden for garnish. "I'll be home around lunch," he promised.

They didn't really expect to sell that much lemonade. The stand was just a cover for the surveillance. Bug wound up drinking a lot herself. It was really delicious. "I've never had lemonade this good," she told Frankie. "I've only ever drunk it from the can."

"Really?" Frankie said. "It's how my mom makes it."

It was the first time Bug had heard Frankie mention his mom, or home, all summer. Sometimes she forgot he didn't live here.

"Do you miss home?" Bug asked.

Frankie's answer was immediate. "Nope."

"Oh." Bug poured herself another cup of lemonade.

"Do you have brothers or sisters?" Bug ventured.

"Yes," Frankie said. "Two brothers."

"Do you miss them?"

Frankie just shrugged.

"What's it like? Ohio?"

Frankie picked up the book. "We should be paying attention."

Though they hadn't intended for the lemonade stand to earn money, business picked up in the late morning as pedestrian traffic on the block increased. They sold two cups to Nigel, the English guy who lived in the brick apartment on the corner. He didn't have change, so he gave them a dollar and let them keep the fifty cents. Then Rory came by with his dogs. He had five of them that he walked all at once, the leashes wrapped around his wrist, his homemade pooper-scooper contraption in his back pocket. (Every time Bug asked for a dog, Mama refused, citing Rory and his pooper-scooper as the reason.) He drank two glasses. Mr. Manheimer, who had to be a hundred years old, came walking by, practically collapsing onto the seat (well, crate) Bug offered. He drank two cups, though when it came time to pay, he patted his pockets and came up with pennies and lint. "Ach. I remember. I was going to cash my social security check." He knocked his forehead with his knuckles. "I pay you on my way home."

Around lunchtime, Phillip came back from teaching. "Looks like your supply is getting low," he said. "I can go get more lemons."

"Can we pick them?" Bug asked. Their morning stakeout had not revealed much about the Hermit House, but Bug had noticed how many lemon trees were in the neighborhood.

"Have at it," Phillip said.

Frankie didn't want to miss anything at the Hermit House, so Bug left him to mind the stand and went around asking some of the neighbors if they could pick a few lemons. Almost all said yes, and they promised to come out later and try the lemonade.

When she got back, Frankie was furiously scrawling in his book. "I saw something," he said. "In the upstairs window."

"Really?"

Frankie nodded.

"What?"

"I don't know, but something. The curtain moved. We should stay and watch."

"We have to go make more lemonade," Bug said. "And Phillip's making lunch."

"But I saw something," Frankie said.

"We'll come back later."

"But we might miss it," Frankie insisted.

"We'll go fast. If we just sit here with no lemonade, it'll be obvious we're spying," Bug said. The truth was, she was hungry, and Phillip was making his special tuna salad sandwiches with the baby pickles he called gherkins, which Bug thought was about the funniest word in the world.

Frankie reluctantly agreed. Back at Phillip's, they squeezed more lemons while Phillip grilled bread for the sandwiches.

"Can we eat outside?" Frankie asked.

"Someone's motivated," Phillip said. But he gave them their sandwiches on paper plates.

They took the now-full pitcher and their sandwiches back to the table. The sun had disappeared behind the clouds, but it was still very hot out.

"It's muggy," Phillip said, buying a cup for himself before he left for his afternoon lessons. "I think it might storm."

"In August?" Bug said. It rarely rained in Los Angeles, and hardly ever in summer.

Frankie and Phillip looked at the sky and at each other and then Phillip finished his drink, placed a dollar on the table, and left.

There was a spurt of business after lunch, but no movement from the Hermit House. The day grew thick with a sticky heat, and business dipped as the streets grew quiet. Hardly anyone seemed to be out. Bug saw Randy jogging up Cabrillo and waved, but he didn't see her. Bug wondered vaguely where Danny was.

The wind picked up, sending leaves and garbage skittering across the pavement, but doing little to cool the afternoon.

Frankie's nose twitched like a rabbit's. "Phillip's right," he said. "It's going to rain."

"It doesn't rain in L.A. in summer," Bug said dismissively.

"Well, it rains in Ohio all the time in summer and it smells just like it smells now." He sniffed again. "Electric."

Bug didn't think electricity had a smell and was about to say so, but then she remembered how Frankie had not questioned her shivery feeling about the Hermit House and decided to keep quiet. This turned out to be a wise call because a few minutes later, the temperature dropped, as if the whole block had caught the Hermit House chill. There was a flash of lightning, followed by a loud crack of thunder, and then it started to pour.

They grabbed Phillip's pitcher and ran, shrieking, back to Bug's apartment. Frankie went upstairs to change while Bug counted the money: Six dollars and fifty cents. Not bad. Enough for two matinee movie tickets.

Frankie returned with a deck of cards. Outside, the trees shook with rain and thunder. Normally, storms like this scared Bug, but this time, with Frankie, she felt safe and cozy.

*A*lmost Summer

PHILLIP WAS GOING AWAY for the night! Bug overheard Mama and him talking about it when he was over watching *Designing Women*, their favorite show after *Moonlighting*.

"When's he going? Does he need us to water the plants?" Bug asked the next morning. Watering Phillip's plants was a complicated process, because first he insisted you stick this prong into the soil that told you if the plant needed water. Bug loved doing the prong.

"Wednesday, and he's only going for one night, so I think the plants will survive," Mama replied.

"Can Frankie stay with us? Have a sleepover?"

"If that's what Frankie wants."

"Of course that's what Frankie wants!" Bug exclaimed. In her head, she began to make all sorts of plans. They could go to the Santa Monica Pier for fish and chips and ride the bumper cars. They could go to the movies. They both wanted to see *Spaceballs*. Frankie could sleep with Danny or on the couch, or the two of them could camp on the living room floor. Or maybe they could sleep upstairs at Phillip's, by themselves.

And best of all, they could investigate at night. Trying to see the Hermit House after dark had proved challenging. The view from Bug's apartment was limited. They'd asked to go to Dixon's a few times to get Bomb Pops as an excuse to investigate, but Mama always sent Danny with them. If they did a sleepover, they could stay up late and sneak outside together once Mama was asleep.

Later that morning, she told Frankie the good news about the sleepover. As Bug explained all the things she thought they would do, Frankie nibbled on a hangnail. Then he yanked off the nail and spat it out. "I'm gonna stay at Hedvig's."

"But you don't have to," Bug said. "You can stay with us."

"I'm gonna stay at Hedvig's," Frankie repeated.

"But you don't have to," Bug repeated. Then she explained about all the possible sleeping arrangements, in case he was shy about a sleepover with a girl.

"I'm gonna stay at Hedvig's," Frankie said a third time.

"Well, that's just stupid!" Tears flooded Bug's eyes, which made her even angrier. When Frankie didn't reply, she added, "And *you're* stupid."

She waited until she was alone in her apartment to let the tears slide down her face. Only she wasn't alone. Danny was there, drinking one of those disgusting shakes he now had for breakfast every day.

"What's eating you?" he asked.

"What do you care?" she shot back.

"I care." He put his hand to his chest, cross-your-heart style. "What's up?"

"Nobody likes me," she whined.

"I like you."

"No, you don't. You dumped me this summer."

"I didn't dump you, Bug. I just wanted to hang out with friends my own age."

"Randy and Duane aren't your age." She paused. "And they used to be my friends too."

"They still are."

"No, they're not. No one is. Not even Frankie."

"I thought you two were cool."

"So did I." She told him about Frankie refusing the sleepover, preferring to stay at Hedvig's. *Hedvig's!* "It's like someone offering you ice cream, but you say, 'No thanks, I'll have broccoli instead.'"

Bug could see that Danny was trying hard not to laugh at this. "Maybe some people prefer broccoli."

"Frankie hates broccoli."

Danny rubbed his chin, something he did a lot now that he had whiskers growing there. "Maybe it's got nothing to do with you."

"What else would it have to do with?" she asked.

Danny shrugged and gulped down the rest of his shake. "Why don't you go get your suit? You can come with me today."

"Really?" Bug didn't intend to sound so eager. "I mean, I won't cramp your style?"

"You won't cramp anything. We can go straight to the beach if you want."

"We can go to Muscle Beach first," Bug said. "You should keep at it. Your muscles are really growing."

When her brother smiled then, he looked not like Daniel, who had muscles and needed space, but Danny. Her Danny. "Thanks," he said.

•••

At Muscle Beach, Bug watched Danny. He had a whole group of friends now, not just Duane and Randy and Vanessa but a bunch of guys. Randy came over and helped Bug on the rings. "You got some catching up to do," he teased, pinching her skinny arms.

"I'm strong," Bug said, flexing a bicep.

"Yeah, but not as strong as your brother," Randy said.

"We haven't seen you much this summer," Vanessa said. "You been hanging out with your little girlfriend?"

"Who? Beth Ann? No, I've been hanging with Frankie."

Frankie, Bug remembered anew, who'd rejected a sleepover date with her to hang out with Hedvig. Hedvig!

Danny didn't spend too long at Muscle Beach, so they had the rest of the afternoon at Tower 19. It wasn't very busy, so Kip climbed down to talk to them for a bit. He and Danny got into a long conversation about surfing, which apparently Danny was learning. "Gotta hook you up with a wet suit, man," Kip said. "That water is frigid even in summer. Can't handle it without my suit."

"I can handle it," Bug boasted.

"Yeah, but everyone knows you're tough as nails."

This pleased Bug.

That day she stayed in the water longer than she ever had. She swam until her fingers and toes pruned and her teeth chattered. Partly because she loved the water, partly because she wanted to prove Kip right about her, but mostly because Danny stayed in the water with her. They dived into the waves and bodysurfed, and when they finally got out, they flopped on their towels, sunning themselves, playing cards, and eating apples and peanut butter just like they had the last two summers.

They stayed at the beach until four, and then went to get ice cream from Bian. After, they ambled up to the shops at the circle on Pacific to check for the new Echo & the Bunnymen album at the record store. Sun-drunk and happy, Bug was kicking a half-torn tennis ball as they headed up Venice Boulevard toward home. It had been a nearly perfect day and now, dinner. Maybe Mama would let them order fish and chips.

Thwack. The ball made a satisfying hollow sound as she kicked it. "Hey, Danny," Bug began.

"Yep?" he said.

She wasn't sure what she wanted to say, other than to thank him, though she didn't want to sound like a baby.

"I was thinking we could have fish and chips for dinner." She licked her lips, imagining the salty, tart vinegar taste, the way the French fries turned delightfully mushy.

"Or tacos . . . ," Danny said. Tacos were Danny's favorite food after pupusas. But you couldn't get pupusas in Venice.

"Yeah, but we had tacos a couple nights ago," Bug said. "We haven't had fish and chips in a while."

Danny didn't answer, and for a minute Bug wondered if she'd ruined the moment somehow by vetoing tacos. But then she saw Danny's eyes fixed on something in the distance. She followed his gaze to the skinheads. A big group of them—including the ones who had hassled them on their way to the Chinese Diner—half a block away.

They were drinking those big bottles of beer and kicking one of the empties around like it was a soccer ball. There was a spray of broken glass in front of them, so it looked like they'd been playing this game for a while. Bug thought Danny was going to do what Mama had done, walk on past, but at the last minute, he swerved right, in toward the canals, away from home. The Venice canals always seemed to Bug like a hidden world, a fairy-tale land, houses and boats and curved bridges, far away from the rest of the neighborhood. Once Bug and Danny were inside, the skinheads seemed a million miles away.

They weren't, of course. Danny maneuvered himself and Bug back out of the canals toward the beach again, and they took the crowded boardwalk home.

They did not speak of it, or of anything, as they made their way back to the apartment. When they got home to find Mama rifling through the freezer for something to heat up and shouting at them not to track sand, they didn't say anything then, either.

Lemonade

THAT NEXT NIGHT, when Frankie had his overnight at Hedvig's, Mama offered to take Bug to see *Spaceballs*. But Bug didn't feel like going. And anyhow, she and Frankie were supposed to go see *Spaceballs* with the money they'd earned from the lemonade stand.

Stupid lemonade stand. The only thing it had accomplished was to turn Bug into a lemonade addict. She went through a jug a day, constantly picking fruit from neighborhood trees. She'd borrowed Phillip's juicer and still hadn't given it back, though that might've been because she hadn't been in his apartment since the thing with Frankie.

Were they in a fight? Bug wasn't sure. And if they were in a fight, who'd started it? She wasn't sure of that, either.

The Midnight Marauder killed again. Mama had to work late Thursday, and Bug was told to go to Phillip's for dinner. Normally she loved going to Phillip's to eat because he was such an amazing cook and often enlisted Bug as an assistant. But when she got up to his apartment, shyly knocking on the door instead of barging in like normal, Frankie was in the kitchen, pounding steak with a mallet to run though the meat grinder for hamburgers, Bug felt angry all over. Pounding the hamburger meat had always been *her* job.

"I saw something, in the Hermit's windows," Frankie whispered, "last night, before the crime."

Bug was torn. On one hand, she was mad at Frankie. On the other hand, this was pertinent information.

"What did you see?" Bug asked in a noncommittal voice, to show she didn't care one way or another.

"Lights were on, and lots of movement."

"How did you see all that?" She glanced at Phillip to make sure he couldn't hear, but he was on the phone. She could tell by his tone he was talking to Mama.

"Look." Frankie craned his head toward Phillip's kitchen window and pointed. Just beyond the tops of the trees, you could make out one of the Hermit's third-floor windows. "If you climb on the counter, you can see more. We have to do more investigating at night."

"Yeah, well, if we'd had a sleepover, we could've done just that, maybe stopped a murder." Bug could not keep the hurt and anger out of her voice. Frankie must have heard it too. His nose went red, and he pounded the meat with extra force.

"I'm going to go make lemonade!" Bug announced, eager to get away from the sudden awkwardness with Frankie.

"What a fine idea," Phillip said, hanging up the phone. Then he smiled at Bug like she was offering something generous, which made her feel worse.

She wound up making a double-sized portion, squeezing the lemons extra hard against the juicer, even though this made the motor work harder. The juice stung the cuts and hangnails that riddled her hands, but she didn't care. Let it hurt. Stupid Frankie!

At dinner, she ate silently, drinking glass after glass of lemonade.

"What's gotten into you tonight?" Phillip asked.

"Nothing," Bug mumbled.

"Hmm," Phillip replied.

She went home as soon as she finished eating. Mama was still at work. Danny was watching a rerun of *Cheers*. He barely said two words to her before going in for one of his showers.

After a few minutes the lemonade caught up with Bug and she had to pee. She knocked on the door, but Danny had locked it.

"Danny, hurry up."

"I just got in," he called. The sound of the water trickling made Bug's need to pee even more urgent.

She pounded on the door. "I gotta go!" she yelled. "Bad!"

"Tough," he said.

"Like emergency bad. I'm gonna pee in my pants."

"Just go upstairs if it's such an emergency," he said.

Bug ran up the stairs to Phillip's apartment and pushed open the door like normal. Phillip was playing piano, and he just smiled and nodded at her. Bug ran past him to the bathroom, feeling the pee dot her underwear as she reached for the doorknob. But it was also locked.

She pounded on the door.

"I'm in here," Frankie called.

"I need to pee," Bug cried.

"But I'm in here," Frankie replied.

"But I need to go. Bad!"

"I'll be done in a minute."

"It's an emergency!" Bug cried.

She heard the sound of the toilet flushing, but by then it was too late. The dam had burst.

She had wet her pants. Like a baby.

She stared at the mess in horror, wanting to run downstairs and hide in her bed, pretend none of this had ever happened. But just then Frankie opened the door. He took one look at Bug's wet shorts, the liquid pooling on Phillip's freshly waxed wood floors. He got a funny expression on his face.

And then he started to laugh.

It was a knife, straight to Bug's heart. Her so-called friend, who had slept over at Hedvig's instead of hers, was now laughing at her.

"I hate you!" Bug cried, turning to run.

"Bug, wait," Frankie called after her.

But she didn't wait. She ran down to her apartment and slammed the door, swearing never ever to see Frankie again.

Sleepover at Beth Ann's

BUG WASN'T SURE what happened next, hiding as she was, in her bed. But Phillip must have told Mama, because when she came home from work that night, she climbed up the ladder and lay down next to Bug.

"What can I do to make it better?" Mama murmured, playing with Bug's hair.

Bug loved it when Mama did that. It usually made her feel warm and tickly inside. But not tonight.

"Hmphh!" Bug said, turning away and burying her head under the pillow.

"Anything you want," Mama said.

Bug peered up. "You can let me play with some of my *real* friends!"

"Frankie is your real friend."

Some friend. "He laughed at me!" Tears of humiliation stung at her eyes. She buried her head once more.

"I'm sure he didn't mean it like that," Mama said, gently removing the pillow.

Why did grown-ups always say things like that? He'd laughed in her face! What else could it mean?

"You said you'd do anything I want," Bug said, sitting up. "I want to play with one of my real friends."

Mama sighed. "Okay, which real friend do you want to play with?"

"Beth Ann," Bug said. She was a real friend, wasn't she? Sure, they rarely saw each other outside of school, but that was because Beth Ann lived in Burbank, which was far, and Mama hated to drive, and Beth Ann's parents wouldn't let her stay in Venice. But at school, the two of them played every day at recess.

"And I want to sleep over," Bug demanded. "At her house."

Mama arranged it for Friday night. Because Burbank was closer to downtown than to Venice, Bug would spend the day at

Mama's office and Mama would drive her after work, or if she had to work late, on her dinner break. Bug knew it was inconvenient—a whole mess of running around, lots of traffic—but she didn't care. In fact, she was hoped there was extra traffic. It would serve Mama right for "saving" her summer with a mean friend who laughed at her. Probably they were all laughing at her.

Mama's office wasn't really an office so much as a desk in a big, noisy room full of other desks, which they called the bullpen. Normally, Bug loved going there. She visited with Mama's coworkers, many of whom kept candy or gum in their desks. Sometimes they let Bug sharpen their pencils or do their Xeroxing of newspaper clippings for them. One time, Bug had even seen the mayor walking through the office. Mama hardly even cared, though. She said that was old news. She only got excited when one of the famous TV newscasters, like Tad Draper, came by. Not because they were famous but because they were reporters.

Mama had a thing for reporters. She'd been studying to become one when she met Bug's father, but she'd had to stop after she got pregnant with Danny. Later, after they moved to Venice, Mama finished her degree. When she'd graduated, the *Herald Examiner* had offered her an internship, which paid a little and had no health insurance, while the mayor's office had offered her a job as an assistant press officer, which paid a salary and did have health insurance. Mama, who'd been scraping by, waiting tables and juggling Bug and Danny with the help of Hedvig and Phillip, said it wasn't even a question. She took the job at the mayor's office and had been there ever since.

At home, they had a stack of videotapes of movies about reporters: *All the President's Men* (boring), *Network* (so many bad words!), and *His Girl Friday* (Bug's favorite). Mama and Bug would watch the movies together sometimes.

"Do you still wish you were a reporter?" Bug would ask her as they watched.

"I wish a lot of things," Mama said. "That's what makes them wishes."

Bug knew that the Midnight Marauder was a big deal—Mama's late nights had been a testament to that—but when she got to the bullpen, she understood just how big this story was. There were blackboards full of information about each of the attacks. There were enlarged maps of the city, kind of like Frankie's, with details on each incident. News clippings from papers all over the country covered four entire bulletin boards!

If Frankie could see this, Bug thought. But then she banished the thought. She no longer cared what Frankie could see.

Mama spent the morning on the phone, while Bug sat on an extra chair next to her desk, pretending to read the diary of Anne Frank but really eavesdropping on Mama's conversations.

Though her and Frankie's investigation was obviously over, Bug wished she'd thought to bring the notebook, just to jot down some of what Mama was saying. Even though a lot of what she was saying was that she couldn't say a lot. "Billy, you know I can't tell you that," Mama told one reporter, a variation on what she'd said to the one before. But with one caller, she gave a bit more information, lowering her voice to an almost whisper. "Off the record? Okay, off the record, we think he's slowing down, getting more cautious, and we credit that to law enforcement's presence, but no one here is breathing until he's in custody."

Slowing down. Getting more cautious. No one's breathing. Bug tried to memorize the words. Then reminded herself she didn't need to anymore. Then did anyway.

Mama paused. And in a quieter voice, "Yes, *dead* would work too."

Dead. Bug made a note of that in her mental notebook.

As if Mama could read Bug's thoughts, she looked up. "Hang on a sec," she said into the phone. She rummaged through her bag for some quarters and instructed Bug to go the vending machine for a soda. Bug didn't want a soda but understood she was being sent away. She took her time getting up, but Mama didn't get back on the phone until she left.

Mama was more careful after that, sending Bug on errands when she had phone calls to make. Bug lingered by the big boards with all the clues written on them. She memorized as much as she could. That afternoon Mama had to go out to a press briefing, and though she sometimes allowed Bug to come with, today she made her stay with a secretary who had Bug sharpen pencils in the electric machine. Once she had enjoyed this—pushing the dull pencil in and pulling it out with a perfectly pointy tip—but today it only made her feel like the stupid kid who couldn't be trusted to know important things.

Finally, it was time to leave. They fought their way through rush-hour traffic to Burbank. When they got to Beth Ann's neighborhood, Bug peered out the windows, looking for movie stars, but didn't see any.

Beth Ann's mom was waiting with a tray of snacks and lemonade (from a can; Bug could taste the difference now). She brought the tray upstairs, where Beth Ann was flopped out on her bed, leafing through a stack of *Tiger Beat* magazines.

"Which Taylor do you like?" Beth Ann asked, holding up a magazine with the band Duran Duran on the cover. "Roger, Andy, or John? Nick Rhodes is mine, so hands off."

The last conversation Bug had with Beth Ann, back in June, had been about the space shuttle. Beth Ann thought women shouldn't be astronauts, because if they exploded like the *Challenger* did, they would die. Bug thought that was dumb. What difference did it make whether you were a girl or a boy if you got blown up?

Beth Ann rolled over onto her back, the magazine held aloft. "Everyone likes Simon Le Bon because he's the singer, so I think I have more of a chance with Nick." She went over to the wall. In the place where a map of the solar system had once hung was a poster of Duran Duran. She kissed the poster, then walked from one end of her room to the other. "His eyes follow me as I walk." She crossed the room again. "Try it," Beth Ann said. Bug took a few steps. Beth Ann was right. The eyes did follow you.

"So," Beth Ann said, when she'd sat back down on the bed. "Which one do you like best?"

Danny had some Duran Duran cassettes from a few years ago, and Bug had seen the video of them on a sailboat on MTV. "I don't know. I don't care."

"How can you not care? They're the most amazing! And not just because they're so cute. Their music, it moves me. Here, listen." She pulled out a single of "Save a Prayer" and played it on her turntable as she did this weird ballet-prance around her room.

Bug watched her, an uneasy feeling taking hold in her stomach. Like she'd been dropped off at the wrong house.

Beth Ann danced a bit more and then they ate the snacks. "What have you been doing this summer?" she asked Bug.

Bug didn't know how to talk about her summer without mentioning Frankie, so instead she talked about the Midnight Marauder, all the information she knew about him, from the pattern of attacks to the yellow houses.

Beth Ann looked bored. She turned back to her magazines.

"You know there was an attack right here in Burbank?" she asked Beth Ann. Maybe that would impress her.

It didn't. Beth Ann wrinkled her nose. "You're so weird sometimes."

●●●

They didn't talk for a while, just listened to the record over and over. Outside, it was starting to get dark, but it stayed much hotter in the San Fernando Valley at night than at the beach, and across the neighborhood, you could hear people still splashing in pools.

"Want to go swimming?" Beth Ann asked.

Bug had forgotten her bathing suit, which was a stupid thing to do.

"That's okay," Beth Ann said. "You can borrow one of mine."

Beth Ann retrieved two suits and proceeded to take off her clothes. She pointed to her chest, which had two cone-shaped mounds on it. "I'm developing. My mom got me a bra!"

Bug's own chest was flat. It had never bothered her before. She turned to face the wall to change into the bathing suit, a feeling of sadness hollowing out her belly. She felt homesick. Which was so confusing, because wasn't home what she'd wanted to get away from?

No Word

MAMA HAD ARRANGED to pick Bug up the next morning, but when the car beeped at ten, it wasn't the scratchy Datsun horn but the more musical honk of the Cabriolet.

"Your mom got a convertible?" Beth Ann asked. It was the first time she'd sounded impressed since Bug arrived.

"No," Bug replied, grabbing her backpack and running out the door, saying thank you to Beth Ann's parents like Mama had taught her to. As she approached the curb, she wondered why Phillip was picking her up instead of Mama. Had there been another Midnight Marauder attack?

When Bug saw who else was sitting in the car, she skidded to a stop. "What's *he* doing here?"

Frankie climbed out of the passenger seat. "I asked to come." He stared at his knees. "I—I want to talk to you."

"You two can sit in the back," Phillip said. "I'll put the top down so you can have privacy." He reached into the glove box for the Grace Kelly scarf.

"Frankie doesn't like the top down," Bug said.

"It's okay," Frankie said.

Bug reluctantly climbed into the backseat while Phillip cranked the canvas roof down. Frankie didn't say anything as they pulled away. Or as they merged onto the freeway. Not until the car climbed to the top of the hill that separated the Valley where Beth Ann lived from the beach where Bug lived did Frankie speak.

"I'm sorry I laughed at you," he began.

"You should be!" Bug shot back, the apology reviving her humiliation.

"I didn't do it to be mean. It was just a nervous reaction."

"Sure it was," Bug scoffed.

"Trust me, I would never do it on purpose. Because I know how it feels." His expression looked anguished.

"To pee in your pants?"

A shadow darkened Frankie's face. "To have to go really bad and not be able to . . ." He trailed off.

"Why? Do your brothers hog the showers too?"

Frankie shook his head and blushed.

"I couldn't unlock the door because I was scared you'd see," Frankie said.

"See what?"

Frankie didn't say anything, only glanced between his legs. Bug might not have understood what he meant had he not turned so red that he looked like a tomato with ears.

"Oh, you mean your private parts?" Frankie nodded. "I mean, I get it," Bug continued, "but you know that I've seen Danny's a bunch of times."

"Mine aren't like Danny's," Frankie said, talking to the floor. "They're like yours."

"Like mine?" Bug was confused. "But I'm a girl."

She looked at Frankie, who looked like he was going to cry. She saw Phillip watching intently in the rearview mirror. And suddenly, she began to understand—the refusal to swim, or sleep over, Mama's various concerned comments—what Frankie was trying to tell her.

"Are you a tomboy?" That was what Aunt Teri called Bug on account of her distaste for dresses and her affection for dirt. But even though she didn't like girly things, she still was a girl.

"I don't think so," Frankie said.

"You don't seem like a girl," Bug said.

"I don't *feel* like one either. I never have."

"Really? Never?"

"For as long as I can remember." Frankie paused to bite his thumbnail. "My mom says God doesn't make mistakes, but my dad says he did with me."

"That's not true!" Bug countered with a wave of indignation. Frankie was brave and loyal and most definitely *not* wrong. She suddenly felt ashamed for how she'd treated him just because he didn't want to sleep over! "You're not a mistake!"

"I don't think I am, but my dad sure thinks so. . . ." His chin wobbled, but he did not cry. "He says I have to quit it."

"Quit what?"

"All of it. Wearing boy clothes, having a boy haircut, going by Frankie, even though no one has ever called me anything else. He says it's time for me to be a girl." Frankie shuddered, and not in the jokey ways boys did when they were compared to girls, but like the prospect truly scared him.

"What about your mom?" Bug asked.

"She has to do what he says."

"Why?"

Frankie considered it. "Because the dad is the boss."

Was that true? Had her father been the boss? Bug couldn't imagine Mama having a boss, except for the mayor, but that was different.

"Anyhow, it was Mom's idea, to send me here for the summer to be with Phillip. He's her brother." Frankie lowered his voice. "My dad doesn't like him, though."

Bug already wasn't too crazy about Frankie's father, but when he said this, she started to really dislike him. Phillip was like the nicest person in the world. What was there not to love?

"My mom told him I should come spend the summer here and"—Frankie paused to swallow—"get it out of my system."

"Can you?" Bug asked. "Get it out of your system?"

"I don't think so." Frankie took a juddering breath. "But I have to. That was the deal we made."

"The deal?"

"I get to be Frankie for one more summer, and then when I go back, I have to stop acting like a sissy."

"A sissy?" Frankie, who didn't cry when rubbing alcohol was poured on his cut, was the least sissy person Bug had ever met. And that included Mama! "You're the opposite of a sissy."

Frankie shrugged. "There's no word for what I am."

Hedvig's Story

THE NEXT MORNING Mama woke Bug up and said she had a surprise.

"They caught the Midnight Marauder?" she asked, trying to keep the disappointment out of her voice. It wasn't like she wanted people to get hurt, but the day before, after she'd apologized for getting mad at Frankie about the sleepover and he'd apologized for laughing at her, they had returned to their investigation. Bug told Frankie all she'd overheard at Mama's office as Frankie took copious notes in the book, nodding every so often and saying, "This is really good stuff."

"What? No," Mama said. "We're going to Disneyland."

"We are?" Bug asked, sitting up in bed. "When?"

"Today."

"Today? Really? Can Frankie come?"

Mama smiled. "Of course he can. And Phillip, too."

Disneyland! Today! With Frankie! Bug clapped her hands in delight. Though they were only an hour's drive from the theme park, Bug had only ever gone once, a few years back, when Aunt Teri had taken her. She had loved it so much, even if she regretted being too scared to go on Space Mountain (and not just because Danny had teased her for being a chicken). She'd made a vow that the next time she went to the park, she would ride it five times in a row. But she had not yet had yet the opportunity to make good on that.

"Is Danny coming?" She was eager to prove to Danny how brave she now was.

"No, he said he's too old for Disneyland," Mama said. "And we only have room for five in the car."

"No one's too old for Disneyland," Bug replied. "And there's only four of us."

"Hedvig's coming," Mama said.

"Hedvig! Why?"

"She's the one who got us the tickets for free," Mama said. "Her son works for Disney."

"But does she even want to come?" Bug asked.

"Oh, yes, she insisted." Mama pulled off the covers and climbed down the ladder. "Now go get dressed."

Mama had set out cereal, but Bug was too excited to eat. She raced to the alley and waited by Mama's car, which they were taking because it had more room than Phillip's. Frankie was already there, even more excited than Bug, apparently.

"I brought snacks," Hedvig called when she emerged a while later, wearing silky turquoise pajamas, white sneakers, and a paisley-patterned turban.

"She looks like a Disney cartoon herself," Frankie whispered to Bug.

"And I brought donuts," Phillip said, shaking the box, a rare treat from Phillip, who preferred homemade things.

Mama drove. Hedvig sat in the passenger seat. Bug sat in back, between Phillip and Frankie, and though she hated the middle seat, with its weird hump, she didn't complain. They were going to Disneyland!

The radio was on, set to KROQ, which was playing an hour of nonstop songs: Oingo Boingo. U2. The Thompson Twins. The Cure. Hedvig sang along to all the songs, making up words when she didn't know them. Phillip sat there expressionless, though

Bug saw his mustache twitch and suspected he, too, was stifling laughter.

When the commercials came on, Mama turned the radio down and Hedvig twisted around in her seat. "Are you excited?"

Frankie and Bug assured her they were.

"Not so excited as me," Hedvig said, tapping herself on the chest. "Disneyland is my favorite place on earth."

"But you're old," Frankie said.

Bug waited for Frankie to get a scolding from Phillip, but Phillip just laughed.

"Yes, but not too old to go to Disneyland. When my Mihály was alive, we went all the time."

"You must really like rides," Frankie said.

"I don't go on the rides," Hedvig replied.

"Then what's the point of going?" Bug asked.

"Let me tell you a story," Hedvig said.

In her head, Bug groaned. Hedvig's stories tended to go on forever.

"I grew up in Hungary. It was the most magical place on earth," Hedvig began. "We lived in Budapest. A city so beautiful you cannot imagine. It is like Sleeping Beauty's castle but a whole city of it. And summers, we went to the Balaton. Like

Tom Sawyer's island, only you can swim in the lake."

"Uh-huh," Bug said. She did not see what this had to do with Disneyland.

"And then the Soviets came," Hedvig continued. "And we fell behind the Iron Curtain."

Bug knew that the Soviet Union was bad and had like a zillion nuclear bombs pointed at America that could blow them all to smithereens.

"We thought we could resist them. The Hungarians rose up. We had a revolution."

"That was in fifty-six, wasn't it?" Phillip asked.

"Yes," Hedvig replied.

"I remember watching it on the news when I first moved out here."

Bug scrambled to do that math. It was 1987 now. Phillip had moved to Venice in 1956, which meant Phillip been living in Venice since Mama was five years old.

"The revolution was not successful," Hedvig said, "and after, the Soviets came down with an iron fist, everything in Budapest became gray. Even the Balaton became gray."

"But it didn't really become gray, right?" Bug asked. She knew the Soviets were bad, but could they erase color?

"No," Hedvig said. "But it seemed that way. The joy was gone from everything. I was married then, only a short time, to my Mihály. We had started a store before the occupation. A clothing boutique. I designed. Mihály sewed. Our clothes were very stylish. When the Soviets came, fashions too became gray."

Bug looked at Hedvig, in her pajamas and turban. She wasn't sure if they were stylish, but they definitely were not gray.

"We decided to defect," Hedvig continued.

"Defect?" Frankie asked.

"It means to sneak out of the country," Phillip explained.

"One summer, we packed like we were going to the Balaton. One suitcase. With bathing suits and sandals, because we did not want to make any suspicion. I could not bring anything else. Not even a picture of my family. Otherwise they could be arrested."

"Arrested? Why?" Frankie asked.

"For aiding us. When we said goodbye, I could not allow myself to cry when I kissed my *anya*, my mother, because she would be suspicious. Then we drove like we were going to the Balaton, but really we went close to the Austrian border. We hid our car in the bushes by the side of the road and walked across the border."

"You couldn't drive?" Frankie asked.

"The borders were closed. We had to sneak across in darkness."

"Like *The Sound of Music*?" Bug asked, enthralled.

"Exactly," Hedvig said. "Only I didn't sing. I cried all night, imagining my beloved *anya* hearing that the car was found. If they told her we defected, she would be under suspicion, but if they didn't tell her, she would think we had died. They might even tell her we had died."

"But that's a lie!" Bug cried.

"Defecting was humiliation for the Soviets, so they hid the truth."

"So what happened?" Bug asked, leaning forward in her seat. The story had started out boring, like something from school, but had turned interesting. Hedvig, who lived downstairs with all that junk, had escaped from the Soviets in the middle of the night. To look at her now, you would never guess. Bug glanced at Frankie. Maybe that was true of lots of people. "Did your mom get in trouble?"

"She did not."

"Did she think you'd died?" Frankie asked.

"She did not know, but she prayed that I'd escaped. It was many years before I was able to get word to her that we were okay in America. And then we could exchange letters, but we had to be careful because the spies read everything."

"Did you ever see her again?" Bug asked.

Hedvig shook her head. "When she became a *nagymama*"—she paused—"a grandmother, we tried to get her a visa, but she got sick and died before she could visit."

"I'm sorry, Hedvig," Mama said, putting a hand on her wrist. "I know how hard that is."

"Did you ever see any of your family again?" Bug asked.

"My cousin," Hedvig replied. "She moved to Dallas. She's who I go visit every August." Hedvig sighed dramatically. "She is the only one left."

Mama squeezed Hedvig's hand.

"That's a good story, but what does it have to do with Disneyland?" Frankie asked.

"Ah, yes. The point of my story. It take us a while to get to America," Hedvig said. "We had to stay in Austria for a year before we finally flew to Los Angeles. We had friends who had come here and they knew us from our shop, so they got us jobs in the wardrobe department for Metro-Goldwyn-Mayer."

"The movie studio?" Bug gasped. "Did you meet famous people?"

"All the time," Hedvig said. "After we start to work and find an apartment, our friends say they want to take us to Disneyland. It only just opened. We had no extra money, but they insist we go as their guests."

Hedvig stopped, like that was the end of the story. It reminded Bug of Hedvig's soap operas, which would have a big cliff-hanger on Friday afternoon—someone getting shot—and you'd wait all weekend to see what happened only to find out no one got killed or arrested or anything good.

But Hedvig's story wasn't over yet. "When I step through the gates of Disneyland, I cried."

"You *cried?*" Bug asked.

"Why?" Frankie asked.

"People cry when they see the Statue of Liberty. Because it means freedom. But I fly to America, and I don't see it. But when I stepped through the Disneyland gates, I cried for the same reason. Because it was America. It was freedom."

Bug didn't say anything. She loved Disneyland, sure, but it seemed a little silly to *cry*. Then again, Hedvig had cried when Luke and Laura had broken up on *General Hospital*.

"I cried when I saw the Pacific," Phillip said. "I was twenty-four years old and it was the first time I'd ever seen the ocean."

Twenty-four in 1956. It was now 1987. Bug paused to count

on her fingers. Fifty-five! Phillip was fifty-five. She filed that away to tell Danny later.

"Why would that make you sad?" Frankie asked.

"I wasn't sad," Phillip replied. "I was the opposite of sad. Full of hope. California was the New World for me, a place to escape a different kind of gray."

"When I moved here from Visalia, I cried all the way down on the bus," Mama said. Bug knew this, of course, but she'd never heard it from Mama, only from Danny, and Danny had never told her what Mama said next. "It was only when I got here that I stopped crying."

"So you both understand," Hedvig said, "what it means to be a refugee."

Magic Kingdom

NOBODY CRIED WHEN they got to Disneyland, but something happened to Frankie. As soon as the tram from the parking lot pulled up to the front gates, his posture changed. His shoulders stopped hunching, his chin emerged from the burrow of his neck. Bug had not realized how curled up he usually was, like a turtle in his shell, until she saw him craning his head every which way.

He wanted to see everything. He wanted to go on everything. Bug may have had a list ranking the rides, but for Frankie, there were no bad rides: the Mad Tea Party, the Haunted Mansion, Space Mountain. All were fantastic. Amazing. Let's do it again. Even the monorail, which wasn't really a ride, Frankie loved. Bug thought Disneyland was fun, but for Frankie it really seemed to be magic.

He'd brought Phillip's camera with him, and he snapped pictures everywhere, even posed with Pluto, which Bug felt was maybe babyish but was glad Frankie was doing it because then she got to also. If Danny laughed at the photos, or at the Mouseketeer hats with their names stitched on them they'd each bought, she'd be able to say she'd done it for Frankie.

They rode rides until lunchtime. When Bug had come with Teri, they'd packed lunches—her aunt said the food prices there were exorbitant—but Phillip and Mama let Frankie and Bug eat at a restaurant near the Country Bear Jamboree: fried chicken and French fries, washed down with a large soda each!

"What now?" Phillip asked.

"Pirates of the Caribbean!" Bug exclaimed. "And I want to do Space Mountain again."

"And I want to do Star Tours again."

"But the line is so long," Bug complained.

"I know, but it's a fun line."

"That's true," Bug agreed.

"If you don't mind," Hedvig said, "I would like to go to Tom Sawyer Island."

Hedvig hadn't made a single request all day, so though Bug felt that, like the monorail or the riverboat, the raft to Tom Sawyer's island did not constitute a ride, she agreed. At least the line wasn't too long.

Over on the island, they climbed around the shore, visited the fort. And then Frankie got a funny look.

"What's the matter?" Bug asked.

"I have to find Phillip," he said.

"Is everything okay?"

He nodded, but his face looked weird. He found Phillip, and Frankie whispered something and Phillip looked around. "Okay, let's just go."

On the raft back, Frankie was dancing from side to side, like really fast. Bug might've thought he was goofing around were it not for the grimace on his face. And that was when Bug realized he had to pee. Now that she thought about it, she had to go too. She'd drunk a lot of soda with lunch.

There was a bank of bathrooms right when they got off the ferry. But Frankie didn't go in those.

"We'll meet you at the Pirates of the Caribbean," Phillip called behind him.

After the bathroom, they went to the Pirates ride. Mama said they could go on without Frankie, but Bug preferred to wait until Phillip and a very relieved-looking Frankie reappeared.

"Where'd you go?" she asked.

"To a handicapped bathroom," he replied.

"Why not just go in the boys' bathroom?"

"I'm not allowed to," he said.

"Says who?" Bug asked.

"My dad." He paused. "Everyone."

"Well, that's just dumb. Who cares where you pee so long as you don't get it on the seat?"

Frankie sighed. "People care."

The rest of the day went too fast, like all best days did. Before Bug knew it, the sky had darkened and it was time for the Main Street Electrical Parade. She had missed it when she'd come with Aunt Teri—whose feet had hurt and who had insisted that six hours in the park was enough—and though she'd felt cheated at the time, now she was glad they hadn't stayed for the parade, because she could not imagine a better way to see it than with Frankie, who lit up as much as the fireworks that rainbowed across the night sky.

After the parade, even Bug had to admit she was getting sleepy. They made their way down Main Street, stopping at the candy store so they could bring Danny back some fudge. The park was getting ready to close. The crowds were streaming out the gates.

"I wish I could live here," Frankie mused.

"Yes," Hedvig said. "In Sleeping Beauty's castle."

Bug had been thinking the exact same thing. But just then she had a different idea. Frankie couldn't live at Disneyland, but why couldn't he live in California? He'd stay with Phillip and never have to go back to his mean family. They could go to school together. They could solve mysteries together. Roller-skate together. Go to Disneyland once a year.

The idea planted itself like a warm ember in Bug's belly as the car rumbled onto the freeway. She would ask Mama about it tomorrow, but now her eyes were drooping. Her head fell onto Frankie's shoulder, his head leaned against hers. They slept that way the whole ride home.

harks!

SOMEWHERE AROUND THE TIME that Bug and Frankie were dreaming their way home from Disneyland, the Midnight Marauder struck again.

"If we hadn't gone to Disneyland, we could've stopped it," Frankie groused the next morning.

"I know," Bug agreed solemnly, though deep down, she would not have traded the day at Disneyland for anything, not even catching a serial killer. It occurred to her now, though, that if they did catch him, maybe Disneyland would let them go whenever they wanted to. Free tickets for life for the heroes.

Frankie wanted to do another lemonade-stand stakeout. But Bug was sick of stakeouts, even a little sick of lemonade.

"Maybe we can find a different way to investigate," she suggested.

"How?" Frankie asked. "You're not allowed in the alley."

"I know. Maybe we should try other leads."

"What leads?"

Just then Danny emerged from his room, yawning. "How was Disneyland?"

"Okay," Bug said, afraid that if she enthused too much about it or showed Danny her mouse ears, he would call her babyish.

"The Midnight Marauder struck again," Frankie said.

"I know," Danny replied. "I heard last night. You wanna go to the beach? Mom left me money to take you and buy you lunch." He held up a note and a ten-dollar bill. "If you pack lunches and let me keep the money, I'll take you twice this week." Danny paused. "Or even three times."

"What do you need the money for so bad?" Bug asked.

"I want to buy a wet suit." He paused. "Whitney's teaching me how to surf."

"Who's Whitney?" Bug asked. Danny didn't answer but his cheeks went pink, so she understood Whitney was a girl. *Danny and Whitney sitting in a tree,* she began in her head, but she didn't say anything because she wanted to show how mature she was.

"Aren't wet suits expensive?" she asked.

"New ones are, but there's an old surf rat who sells used suits out of the back of his van. And if I can keep this ten, I'll have enough for the one I want. But we gotta go soon because I have Spanish lessons this afternoon. So, are you in or not?"

"Not," Frankie said.

Danny sighed in frustration, because now he wouldn't be getting his wet suit. Bug, who now understood why Frankie didn't want to go to the beach, was not cross with him. But she wanted to find a solution, because she really did want to go to the beach. And, unwittingly, Danny had just given her an idea that would solve *all* their problems.

She followed Danny back into his room. "I have a proposition," she said, using a grown-up word she'd heard on the soap operas.

"Oh yeah?"

"You can keep Mama's money, and I'll tell her we went to the beach, even if we don't. And you can get your wet suit."

"What's the catch?"

"You have to take me with you so I can get a wet suit for Frankie."

"But Frankie doesn't even like the beach."

"He will if he has a wet suit." Bug was sure of this.

"*Frankie* wants to learn to surf?"

"Duh, no."

"Then why does he want a wet suit?"

It was then that Bug understood that Danny did not know about Frankie. For once, she knew something her brother did not! She desperately wanted to lord this over him, but she knew she couldn't. It wasn't up to her to tell Danny, or anyone, about Frankie. It was up to Frankie.

"He wants a wet suit because . . . ," Bug replied, giving herself time to figure out why Frankie might need a wet suit. "The water's too cold for him," she said. "That's why he doesn't like to swim. So do we have a deal?"

Danny stuck out his hand. "We have a deal."

She didn't say anything to Frankie. She wanted it to be a surprise. She just told him she'd be back in an hour. Then she went into her room and collected all the money they'd made from selling lemonade plus everything she had in her piggy bank.

The surf rat moved around, Danny explained, because you weren't allowed to sleep in your van, but he mostly sold his wares in front of the wooden pier that separated Venice from Marina del Rey, the fancier neighborhood to the south.

"How much is the wet suit you want?" she asked Danny.

"Forty bucks."

That was a lot of money. Bug had six fifty from the lemonade stand and three dollars from various tooth-fairy visits and almost four dollars in saved allowance money and nearly fifty cents scavenged from the sofa cushions. Altogether it came to fourteen dollars.

As they approached the pier, Bug crossed her fingers and toes that the surf rat would be there and would have a wet suit she could afford.

The van was there, the shades drawn, the doors locked. Danny knocked on the side window but there was no answer. He shook his head. "Maybe he's out surfing. We can come back."

But just then the creaky door slid open. The surf rat emerged, yawning. "Dude, what time is it?" he asked, squinting at the sun. He was very tan, his skin looked like leather, his blond hair matted into thick dreadlocks.

"It's twelve forty-seven," Bug said, reading the number off Danny's Casio.

"Twelve forty-seven on what day?" he asked.

"Monday," Bug replied.

"Missed the morning swell." He rubbed his eyes. "There's always tomorrow." He looked at Danny. "Oh, hey, dude. You here for that suit?"

"Yes," Danny said. "I have the money."

"Cool, cool." He clambered into the back and returned with a Rip Curl.

"Do you have any smaller ones?" Bug asked. "And cheaper ones?"

The surf rat eyed her. "Who are you?"

"I'm Bug."

"Bug," he laughed. "Cool, cool. My name's Turtle."

"Is that really your name?"

"Is Bug really your name?"

It wasn't. Not really. But what was a name if not the name you thought of yourself as? "Well, Turtle. I'd like your cheapest, smallest wet suit, please."

"You don't want it too small," Turtle said. "You need a bit of space between you and the water. That's how a wet suit works, lets in a layer of water."

"But the water is freezing," Bug said.

"Only at first," Turtle said. "Your body temperature warms

it up right quick. Though I always hold my morning piss and then once I paddle out, I let it rip." He smiled. "It's like a warm bath."

"Eww," Bug said, wondering why anyone would intentionally do what she'd done by accident. But then she remembered what Phillip said about flies and honey. "Sorry."

"No need," Turtle said. "Urine is sterile. Lot of people don't know that. Now let me see what I can find for you."

"It doesn't have to fit exactly right."

"Yeah, it does, or the water won't warm."

"I don't care about that," Bug said.

"I thought Frankie didn't like the cold," Danny said.

"Right," Bug replied, getting caught up on her own fibs.

"Hold on." Turtle disappeared into the van, closing the door behind him. They could hear him moving things around. It sounded like he had a lot of stuff back there.

He emerged with a bright blue Ocean Pacific shortie with a rip up one of the legs. "My pal Jamie got snagged on a nasty piece of coral in Mexico. You should see the scar. Gnarly. She tells people it was a great white and they buy it. Anyhow, I was gonna try to repair it, but if you wanna buy it, I'll let you have it for cheap."

"How cheap?"

"I dunno. Twenty bucks."

"But it's ripped."

"That's why it's cheap."

"I only have fourteen dollars."

Turtle scratched his chin.

"Please," she said. "It'll make my friend so happy."

He continued scratching his chin. Then he smiled, a big gappy grin. It looked like it had been a long time since he'd seen a dentist.

"I can work with fourteen."

Bug ran all the way home, hugging the wet suit, imagining the look of happiness on Frankie's face when she showed it to him.

But he barely looked up from the notebook when Bug presented the wet suit with a dramatic "Ta-da!"

"Thanks," he said absently.

"Now you can go to the beach!" she declared.

"I don't want to go to the beach."

"But I got you a wet suit! It cost fourteen dollars. I had to use my tooth-fairy money and all the lemonade money."

Frankie frowned. "That was *our* money."

"But I used it to buy something for you!" Bug exclaimed.

"You didn't ask me if I wanted a wet suit."

"I wanted to surprise you."

"No, you wanted to go to the beach, and you can only go if I go."

"I want you to *want* to go, and I didn't want you to worry about bathing suits and stuff."

Frankie's face went all scrunchy. "*That's* not why I don't want to go swimming."

"It's not?" Bug was confused. "Why don't you want to go, then?"

"I just don't," Frankie said in a wounded tone that made Bug feel like she'd done something wrong, even though she hadn't. She'd used her money to buy him a wet suit! Frankie was just a stupid booger and still refused to go to the beach. It wasn't fair!

They hardly talked for the rest of the afternoon, and Bug wondered if they were in another fight, and if so, why? She hadn't done anything wrong! She tried to do something nice. Frankie was being dumb! But, like a worm in an apple, there was this niggling feeling pushing up that whispered maybe she *had* done something wrong.

That night, she was in her pajamas when Frankie knocked at the door.

"I'm sorry about the wet suit," she said at the same time Frankie said, "I'm scared of sharks."

"What?" Bug asked.

"I watched all the *Jaws* movies, and I'm terrified of sharks. I have nightmares about them."

"Sharks?" It took Bug a minute to understand. "*That's* why you don't want to go in the water?"

"It's like seventy percent why. I also want to investigate the Hermit." Frankie looked down. "And maybe a little of what you thought."

"Sharks aren't a weird thing to be scared of." Bug paused. "I'm scared of octopuses. I have a dream sometimes that a pink one is in my closet. I know that sounds dumb."

Frankie shuddered. "No, it sounds scary."

That made Bug feel better. "There aren't sharks at Venice Beach." She paused. "Or octopuses."

"Are you sure? I read in Phillip's encyclopedia there were."

"Mama," Bug called. Mama looked up from the dining table, where she was just now eating the pupusas Danny had brought home earlier.

"Yes, Bug," Mama answered.

"Are there sharks in the ocean here?"

"Not the kind that bite people," she said.

"Are you sure?" Frankie asked.

"I work for the mayor's office," Mama replied. "If there were great white shark attacks, I would know. And if there were great white shark attacks, I would not let any of you go in the water."

"Really?" Frankie asked.

Mama sighed and took a swig of her beer. "Trust me. Sharks are the last thing you have to worry about."

The Beach Day

THE NEXT MORNING Frankie appeared at Bug's door wearing his wet suit and carrying Phillip's cooler. "Submarine sandwiches, homemade chocolate chip cookies, and potato salad," he announced. "Phillip packed us lunch," he added, unnecessarily because who else made such a feast on a regular Tuesday?

Just when the day didn't seem like it could get any better, Danny appeared, even though it was not yet ten in the morning. "Let me shower," he said. "And then we'll get going."

Who showers before the beach? Bug thought, but she held her tongue. She was realizing you didn't always have to say the things you thought. She didn't even balk when Danny asked if he could stop by Muscle Beach first.

"Of course," she said, enjoying how magnanimous she felt. She turned to Frankie. "If it's okay by you."

"Sure," Frankie replied.

The whole gang was there, and they greeted Bug and Frankie warmly. "Where have you two been?" Randy asked, as he pushed himself up and down on the parallel bars.

"Have you found any clues about the Midnight Marauder yet?" Duane asked, midway through a sit-up.

"We have a suspect," Frankie said.

"You do?" Randy leapt off the bars.

"Who?" Danny asked.

"The Hermit," Bug admitted. She waited for Danny to laugh at her or call her foolish, but instead he just nodded. Maybe he too had learned to think things instead of saying them. Or maybe he didn't think it was such a crazy idea.

"Who's the Hermit?" Randy asked, his leg jumping up, down, up, down. He was always moving like that. He reminded Bug of the Energizer Bunny from the battery commercials.

Frankie pulled out the book and explained that the Hermit

was, well, a hermit. That he lived alone in the big house, and that his car tended to move on the nights of attacks.

"He's a Vietnam veteran," Danny said. "Came back from the war not right in the head."

"How'd you know that?" Bug asked.

"Mom told me."

"Lotta guys came back from Nam not right in the head," Bill said knowingly. "That kinda violence does something to a person."

Frankie nodded solemnly.

"You two keep at it," Vanessa said. "And we'll get back to making sure we can take him on once you get proof."

Frankie put away the notebook, and he and Bug retreated to a bench half-shaded by a palm tree. They watched the exercisers and then, when that got boring, they watched the boardwalk. Zeus was out with his boom box, skating with a group of people, each one taking a turn at the center of the scrum in a sort of skate dance-off.

Bug and Frankie walked over to watch. The tricks were impressive, spins and leaps. At one point, a very tall, very dark-skinned skater wearing a spangled unitard and a hot-pink wig took the center. Frankie gasped. At first Bug thought he was reacting to the outfit, but then she heard the skater say something to Zeus in a baritone voice.

"Oh, it's a man," she remarked to Frankie. This was not that unusual. Venice had all sorts of people dressing up in all sorts of ways.

Frankie just kept staring at the skater, which Bug thought was a little rude, but she kept that opinion to herself. And anyhow, after a while the pink-haired skater caught Frankie's eye and winked. Frankie lit up with a high-beam smile.

They watched the skaters so long that Danny came to fetch them. "You ready to hit the beach?"

"Am I ever!" Bug said.

She expected Frankie to be tentative in the water, given his fears of sharks and being from Ohio, where they didn't have oceans, just Great Lakes, but Frankie ran in without hesitating, same as she and Danny did, whooping, like they always did when the first shock of cold licked at their skin.

Bug showed him how to dive into a wave without getting water up your nose. Frankie's fearlessness should not have surprised her, but seeing him carefully eyeing the waves, then plunging under, like he'd been doing this all his life, made Bug admire him all over again.

When they got tired of ducking waves, they swam past the breakers and treaded water. "Let me know if you get tired," she said.

"I will," Frankie said. "But the wet suit makes it easier to float."

"Really?"

Frankie nodded, flipping onto his back, arms in a T. "This is the life."

Bug couldn't agree more. "I love summer," Bug proclaimed. "Don't you?"

"I love *this* summer," Frankie replied, still floating.

"What about other summers?" she asked.

"They were kinda boring."

"What would you do in Ohio?"

"I don't know. I'd just sit around, build with Legos, or play softball."

"Do you have lots of friends?" Bug asked.

Frankie dunked under the water and popped back up. "I play with people from school," he said. "But they're not really friends." He cupped his hands and squirted water. "Mostly I play with my brothers."

"Me too. Well, until this summer anyhow."

She could hear the hurt in her voice, and maybe Frankie could too, because he asked, "What happened?"

"Danny needed space." Bug stared at her pruney fingers. "From me."

Bug waited for Frankie to tell her she was taking it too personal or that Danny was just at an age. But he didn't say either of those things. He looked at her solemnly, like he understood how bad it hurt when someone you loved didn't want you around. Then he gave his head a little shake. "His loss is my gain," he said.

By now, Bug understood that Frankie had not been brought out to rescue her summer. But at that moment, it sure felt like he had.

9 Don't Knows

THAT FRIDAY NIGHT, Phillip was going away again, and this time Frankie would sleep over. Mama, who'd been working late all week, made good on her promise to come home at a normal time. She took Bug and Frankie to the Santa Monica Pier, where they rode the bumper cars three times and ate a dinner of hot dogs and fresh potato chips, which came out of the oil crispy, chewy, and perfectly salty.

On the way home, Mama let them rent a movie from the video store and didn't balk when they chose *Poltergeist*, even though Bug had had bad dreams for weeks after seeing it the first time. But that was when she was little. She was braver now.

They spread sleeping bags on the living room floor, popped

popcorn, and put the tape in the VCR. The movie was pretty scary, but with Frankie by her side, and Mama yawning in her chair, it was a delicious kind of scary.

After it ended, Mama said she was going to bed and told them not to stay up too late. "We won't," they promised, trying not to giggle. They had already planned it. As soon as Mama was asleep, they would sneak up to Phillip's apartment and climb on the counter and surveil the Hermit House all night long. And, they agreed, if they saw him leave, they would call the police.

As they snuggled under their sleeping bags and recounted their evening, Bug felt warm and happy. This was how it had been with Danny, before he needed space and became Daniel. But it had never felt this way with anyone else.

"Frankie," she whispered, "I think you're my best friend."

"I think you're mine, too," Frankie said in a drowsy voice.

A best friend. Not a friend like Beth Ann, who made Bug feel lousy a lot of the time, or a friend like Bian, who she only saw for a few minutes here and there. But a best friend. She'd waited her whole life for this.

Which made it all so unfair! Because in a few weeks Frankie was going back to Ohio and she was going to lose her best friend.

Unless . . . Frankie lived here. The idea had been bouncing around in the back of her mind since Disneyland, but now she really began to imagine it. Sleepovers every weekend. Trips to the beach. Roller-skating parties and lemonade stands. Bug would even learn to play softball if he wanted to join a team together. That was what best friends did.

"Frankie," she began sleepily.

"Hmm," Frankie said, his eyelids fluttering.

"You should live in Venice," she said. "Forever."

"Uh-huh," Frankie said, and then yawned and rolled over.

"Is that a yes?" It sounded like a yes, but she wanted to hear the word. But Frankie had fallen asleep. "We're supposed to be watching the Hermit," Bug said before falling asleep next to him.

Bug was dreaming of the scary pink octopus in the closet when she heard the front door open. She sat up and saw Mama there, taking the keys from the hook.

Was Mama going to work? Bug's brain was fuzzy, but she thought it was still the weekend.

"Where are you going?" she asked.

"Nowhere," Mama whispered. "Go back to sleep."

Bug blinked and the clock on the VCR came into focus. It was 3:14. Mama never left for work this early.

"Is it the Midnight Marauder?" Bug asked.

"No, baby. Nothing like that. I'll see you in the morning."

Bug wanted to ask more, but she was so tired, and she fell immediately back to sleep. When she woke up again, she thought maybe it had all been a dream. But then she saw that Danny, who never got up before her, was already awake.

Bug rubbed her eyes and looked around. "Where's Mama?"

Danny put his finger over his lips and gestured for Bug to follow him into Mama's room. The bed was empty and unmade. Mama always made her bed, even on weekends.

"Where is she?" Bug asked, the panic rising in her.

"With Phillip."

Bug's mind spun. Phillip was upstairs. Only he wasn't, Bug remembered. He'd gone away, which was why Frankie was here.

"Where's Phillip?"

"In the hospital."

"What? Why?"

"I don't know."

"Is he okay?"

"I don't know."

Bug sometimes fretted about things happening to Mama, or to Danny, and usually she had to scrunch her eyes shut and push the worries away. Because it was just too scary to contemplate. They were all she had.

But now she realized that wasn't true. She had Phillip, too. And something bad had happened to him.

Tears filled her eyes. She waited for Danny to tell her not to be a crybaby, but he blinked hard, as if he was holding back tears of his own.

"What do we tell Frankie?" Bug asked.

"I don't know." Danny put his head in his hands. "I'm sorry, Bug, but I just don't know."

They decided to let Frankie sleep. Maybe by the time he woke up they'd have more to offer than I don't knows. They stayed in Mama's room and turned on the TV, watching Saturday morning cartoons, pouring dry bowls of Lucky Charms like they used to. Danny gave Bug all his marshmallows, but she wasn't hungry enough to eat them.

Frankie was still sleeping when there was a knock on the door. Bug prayed it would be Mama and Phillip, laughing, this whole thing a giant misunderstanding like on *Three's Company*. But it was Hedvig. In tears.

"Phillip has been attacked!" she announced.

In the taxi to the hospital, Frankie barely said a word. Bug held his hand and closed her eyes and prayed. Bug knew you were supposed to pray to God, but whenever anything was really important, it wasn't a bearded man she spoke to, but the familiar-but-not picture in the photo albums. And as they drove to the hospital, she prayed to her father, harder than she'd ever prayed for anything: *Please don't let Phillip die too.*

Phillip wasn't dead. Or in a coma. But he had been bludgeoned.

"He has three broken ribs, and one punctured his lung," Mama reported from the hospital corridor. "But the doctors got that inflated again. And his face is pretty banged up, but thankfully, there's no concussion."

"Who did this?" Hedvig asked.

"Was it the Midnight Marauder?" Frankie and Bug asked in unison.

"No, it was not the Midnight Marauder," Mama said.

"How do you know?" Hedvig asked. "He has been attacking people all over the city. Right?" She looked to Frankie and Bug for confirmation.

"It wasn't the Midnight Marauder," Mama replied. "Phillip was mugged."

"Mugged?" Bug asked. "What's that mean?"

"When you are robbed, violently," Mama replied.

"I thought he was going away," Bug said.

"It happened before he left," Mama said.

"What did they steal?" Bug asked.

"His wallet. Enough questions," Mama said in the firm voice she used when she'd had enough of nosy reporters.

"So, all this for a man's wallet?" Hedvig asked, shaking her head. "Disgraceful."

"That's the word for it," Mama said.

They weren't allowed to go into his room, but after what felt like ages, they were allowed to wave from the door. Phillip was up, in bed, which was good, but his face was swollen and puffy, covered in bandages.

Mama gave Bug ten dollars and sent her and Frankie to the cafeteria to get some lunch. They went by themselves, which was kind of scary and kind of exciting.

"We could get ice cream for lunch and no one would know," Bug said.

Frankie didn't answer. He was subdued. "Phillip's going to be okay," Bug insisted. "On *St. Elsewhere*, once people are awake, they don't die."

Frankie said nothing. So Bug added, "It's a TV show, about a hospital."

They got into the cafeteria line and Bug was suddenly ravenous. She ordered a burger and fries. She wanted a chocolate milkshake, too, but they only had ten dollars. "What do you want?" Bug asked.

"Nothing," Frankie replied.

"Nothing?"

"I'm not hungry."

Bug felt bad about being hungry, like it meant she wasn't worried enough. So she went without the shake. They walked over to an empty table and sat down. All around them were doctors in white coats and nurses in scrubs, and it really did feel like she was in an episode of *St. Elsewhere*.

"Are you okay?" Bug asked him.

She knew it was a dumb question. She'd almost cried thinking about something bad happening to Phillip, and they weren't even related. But she wasn't sure what else to say.

Frankie picked at a hangnail on his thumb until it tore off. Finally he looked up and said, "I have to catch him."

"The Midnight Marauder?"

"No," Frankie replied. "Whoever did this to Phillip. I have to catch him. That's more important now. It's personal."

If she were honest about it, Bug had never truly believed they were going to catch a serial killer. Sure, it would've been great, them heroes, on TV, free lifetime passes to Disneyland. But they were a couple of kids. And the Hermit, scary as he was, had lived there for years, so why start murdering now?

She couldn't tell if Frankie had ever really believed they'd catch the Midnight Marauder either. But by the way he was looking at her now, his eyes pinpoint focused, his mouth set into a grim line, Bug understood that this time he meant it. Because this time it was Phillip. And though she wasn't entirely confident they could do this, he was her best friend. So she summoned her courage and said, "We'll catch him together."

•••

After lunch, Mama drove everyone home.

"What about Phillip?" Frankie asked.

Mama laid a hand on his shoulder. "They want to keep him for observation for a few days."

"You'll stay with us," Bug said to Frankie, to preempt any discussion. But then she remembered what he'd told her about asking what he wanted, not assuming, and added, "If that's okay with you."

Frankie nodded. But when they got back to the apartment, he kept walking up the staircase when they reached their door. Bug started to object, but Mama shook her head. "Give him some time alone."

Inside their apartment, Danny was pacing.

"He's fine," Mama said.

"Really?" Danny asked, looking to Bug for confirmation, which made her feel very grown-up.

"He was awake," Bug said. "They're keeping him for observation."

"He'll be home in a few days," Mama said. "So there's no use sitting inside worrying."

Danny went to his bedroom to change into his wet suit. Mama put on a pot of coffee. It was then that Bug realized it was Saturday and they had not gone to the Chinese Diner. With everything else going on, this shouldn't matter, but somehow, it did.

Mama poured her coffee and let out a heavy sigh. Bug sat down next to her, putting her hand over Mama's. "Phillip's going to be okay," she said.

Mama smiled wearily. "I know that, baby. But thank you for telling me."

"Do you want to watch a movie?" Bug asked. *"All the President's Men?"* That movie, which was all about reporters investigating a president, was super boring, but it was one of Mama's favorites, and today Bug would watch just about anything to make Mama look less sad.

"Maybe later," Mama said. "After I talk to Frankie."

"About what?"

Mama sighed again. "About going home."

For a brief moment, Bug thought Mama had had the same idea as Bug. That Frankie shouldn't go back. That he should stay here and make Venice his home.

But then she saw Mama's face. The faint lines around her eyes more etched than usual, the sadness, always there, more obvious than usual. And that was how Bug understood what Mama meant. Not that Frankie didn't have to go home, but that he had to go home early.

"No!" Bug cried. "You can't send him back!"

"What choice do we have?" Mama said. "Phillip can't take care of him."

"So? Frankie can stay with us. He can have my room. I'll sleep on the floor. We won't go outside. We'll stay in all day and watch soap operas with Hedvig."

Mama shook her head. "Hedvig is going to visit her cousin in Texas on Monday."

"Then we'll sit in our apartment. We won't go outside." Bug swallowed hard. She would do anything to keep Frankie from having to leave early. "I won't even ask to go to the beach."

"Baby," Mama replied. "With everything that's going on, I have to work all the time. And now Phillip's laid up. And Hedvig's going away." She shook her head. "I don't see any other option."

"Then you're not looking hard enough!" Frankie had three weeks left in Venice, maybe more if Bug could figure out how to make that happen. He couldn't go back early.

"None of this is Frankie's fault!" Bug said, the tears she'd been bottling all day finding release. "Not the Midnight Marauder, or what happened to Phillip. None of it!"

"I know, baby," Mama said. "Sometimes life isn't fair."

"You always say life isn't fair and that the most you can hope for is that it's just," Bug said. "Frankie going back early isn't either!"

Bug had never really got what Mama meant by her whole fair/just thing. It was another one of those baffling things grown-ups said. But when Mama sucked in her breath, raised both eyebrows, and said, "I'll figure something out," Bug wondered if maybe she did understand it after all.

Aunt Teri

MAMA'S WAY OF *figuring something out* was Aunt Teri. When she arrived that Monday, Bug went with Mama, who had taken the morning off work, to pick her up from the bus station. Mama had offered to pay for a taxi, but Aunt Teri had refused, so Mama had to drive from Venice to downtown, back to Venice, and then back downtown again for work.

"A taxi?" Aunt Teri *tsk*ed to Bug as they walked from the bus station to the parking lot, Mama lagging behind them under the weight of Aunt Teri's flowered suitcase. "For all I know, the driver could be the Midnight Marauder."

"It's daytime, Aunt Teri," Bug said. "The Midnight Marauder only strikes at night."

"Well, you can't be too careful." She got into the car and tried to lock all the doors. The front passenger door only locked from the outside, so she made Mama get out of the car and lock it for her. "I can't believe you still have this clunker."

"Me neither," Mama replied.

"If you lived somewhere less expensive, you could have a nicer car." She turned to Bug. "I used to have the sweetest Mustang—1968, cherry red."

This Bug knew. Aunt Teri talked about her cherry-red Mustang. A lot.

"What are you waiting for?" she asked Mama. "Let's go before we get attacked."

"My office is a mile away, Teri," Mama said. "And no one's attacked me yet."

"'Yet' being the operative word."

They pulled out onto the street and drove through Skid Row on the way to the freeway. Aunt Teri clucked her tongue at all the homeless people pushing shopping carts full of their belongings. "I don't understand how you can live in this cesspool."

"There's poverty everywhere," Mama said. "Even in Visalia."

"Yes, but they're not roaming the streets like wild dogs. Your mayor should just put them all in jail."

"For what crime?" Mama asked. "Being poor?"

"Oh, I'd imagine you'd have plenty of crimes to choose from. They look like the criminal element."

Mama started to say something but then sealed her mouth into a grim line.

Aunt Teri turned around in her seat so she was facing Bug. "Wouldn't you rather come live somewhere cleaner? With no criminal element. And no serial killer."

"Teri, please don't," Mama said.

Aunt Teri ignored her. "Wouldn't you?" she repeated. "You could have your own room."

"I have my own room now," Bug said.

"What, that closet?" She turned to Mama. "Why don't you come home already? Get a job in Visalia. It's been ten years. Water under the bridge."

"The bridge is burned, Teri," Mama said in a quiet voice.

Bug perked up, not quite sure what they were talking about, only knowing it was important.

"But your kids should be with family," Teri said. "Think of how much easier it would be if you had three adults to look after them."

"We have three adults to look after us," Bug said.

"Who?" Aunt Teri demanded.

"Mama, Phillip, and Hedvig."

Aunt Teri snorted, as if Bug had just proved her point. "They're not family."

When they got home, Mama carried Aunt Teri's bag into her bedroom. Mama would be shifting up to Phillip's apartment with Frankie until he got out of the hospital. Then Mama left for work, promising to be home on the early side if there was no new emergency. No sooner did she leave than Aunt Teri started cleaning.

"You don't have to do that," Bug said.

"Someone does."

"We clean together every other Sunday," Bug said. It was a condition of their allowance money.

"Twice a month," Teri huffed. "No wonder."

"But we cleaned yesterday."

"Never can be too careful or too clean, is my motto," Aunt Teri said.

This sounded like a terrible motto to Bug.

Aunt Teri didn't exactly say Bug had to clean, but she frowned at Bug for sitting in a corner and reading, even though it was for school, so, reluctantly, Bug got a roll of paper towels and a bottle of Windex and cleaned the windows she had just cleaned the day before.

Around lunchtime, Frankie came downstairs, asking if Bug could go play tetherball at the playground. They had planned to meet there to discuss their Phillip investigation.

"Oh, no, missy," Aunt Teri said, pulling the refrigerator out from the wall and frowning at the dust bunnies. "You're not going anywhere."

"The playground is just across the street," Bug said. "I'm allowed to go."

"Not while I'm here." Aunt Teri set down a bottle of 409. "When I'm finished cleaning, we can make a list of activities that are safe."

"And the tetherball court isn't safe?"

"No."

"What about the beach?"

"Certainly not."

It was Bug's habit to protest. But knowing Teri had come so Frankie could stay, she kept quiet. So she picked up the spray bottle and handed Frankie the paper towel rolls. "We can talk while we clean," she whispered.

They'd only just begun discussing their plan to catch Phillip's attacker when Aunt Teri began interrogating Frankie.

"You're here for the summer?" she asked.

"Yeah."

"And your parents allowed you to stay with Phillip?" she asked.

"Yeah."

"And they know . . . everything?"

Frankie and Bug exchanged a look. Which *everything* was Aunt Teri referring to? The serial killer, which they must know about? Frankie's secret, which Bug had not told Aunt Teri about? Or what had happened to Phillip, which they had decided not to tell Frankie's parents about?

"They know everything," Bug said.

It was Monday night, so Danny had brought home pupusas for dinner. Frankie pushed his food around the plate, reminding Bug of that first night when they'd eaten shrimp on the lanai, though Bug knew Frankie didn't have any problem with pupusas. And he now loved shrimp.

Aunt Teri was also pushing around the meat inside the

cornmeal pancake, frowning at the oniony curtido relish that Bug ate by the spoonful. "What is this?"

"Pupusas," Danny said. "Salvadoran food."

"Is this some kind of joke?"

"What joke?" Bug asked.

"You know I don't like this kind of food. And yet you bring it in on my first night."

"We always have pupusas on Monday," Bug explained. "Danny gets them from the Salvadoran area, where he has Spanish lessons."

"*Es la verdad*," Danny said, which only made Teri frown more.

"You know I can't handle spice," Teri said.

"They're not spicy," Mama said.

Aunt Teri wrinkled her nose.

Frankie and Bug exchanged a look, and then Frankie took a big bite of pupusa. "Not spicy at all." Bug felt a warmth flutter in her chest, because she knew Frankie was eating to stand up for her. "And I would know," he added. "Because I'm from Ohio."

Aunt Teri pushed her plate away. "I come all this way to help you and you can't even get food I like," she said, standing up. "I'll go make a baloney sandwich. If you have something as normal as baloney."

"We have baloney," Mama said. "I'll fix you a sandwich."

"I can do it myself," Teri said snippily.

Mama said nothing. Just got that look on her face that she wore every time Aunt Teri came, and Bug remembered, belatedly, how unpleasant Aunt Teri's visits usually were.

When they finished eating, Mama wrapped up the leftovers. "I'm going to bring these to Phillip," she said. "The hospital food is not up to his standards."

"Can I come?" Frankie asked.

Mama thought a moment. Frankie had not been permitted to see Phillip yet. Not the hospital's rules, but Phillip's. He claimed he was not fit for company.

"Please," Frankie added.

"Okay," Mama said.

"Can I come too?" Bug asked. Danny was always out skating with Whitney at night. Bug did not want to be alone with Aunt Teri.

Mama shook her head. "I don't think so."

It's not fair. The thought flickered through Bug's mind. But she let it pass. Frankie was here. And for now, that was what mattered.

*L*ifestyles of the Rich and Famous

FRANKIE CAME HOME from the hospital with some perplexing news. Phillip's wallet, which had been stolen in the mugging, was right there, on the nightstand. "With credit cards and cash and everything," Frankie whispered.

"How did he get it all back so soon?" Bug asked.

"That's just it. I don't think it was ever stolen in the first place. Suspicious."

"You know what else is suspicious?" Bug replied. "Phillip was supposed to be going away, but he got attacked here. Mama said it was before he left, but it was at night."

"Why would they lie?" Frankie asked.

Bug thought about the tone Mama had used at the hospital,

the way she'd spoken to Bug like she was a reporter. "Because there's something they don't want us to know."

The next day Bug and Frankie had planned to meet upstairs after breakfast to start their investigation into what had happened to Phillip. Aunt Teri, however, had a different idea.

"Where do you think you're going?" she asked Bug.

"Upstairs," Bug said. "To Phillip's apartment."

"No sirree bob," Aunt Teri said.

"But it's not outside," Bug protested. "And not nighttime. I'll be fine."

"You're not going into that man's apartment," she replied. "Who knows what you'll catch!"

Phillip's apartment was, like, a hundred times cleaner than theirs, and Bug was sure that there were no dust bunnies hiding behind his fridge, but when she pointed that out, her aunt remained unmoved. "I have a list of fun things we can do."

"Like what? Disneyland? Universal Studios? Knott's Berry Farm?"

Aunt Teri shook her head. "I thought we might do a Lifestyles of the Rich and Famous tour."

"What's that?" Bug asked.

"It's a bus tour of fancy houses. Movie stars, mostly, but apparently there's a shah from Iran who turned his house in Beverly Hills into a Persian castle. It has an indoor racing track and an Olympic-sized pool cut in half, one part for family, and the other for his harem. So the brochure says."

"What's a harem?" Bug asked.

"Never you mind."

"Wouldn't you rather go on rides than sit on a boring old bus?"

"No," Aunt Teri said. "And the house tour is in Beverly Hills. We'll be safe there. The Midnight Marauder wouldn't dare attack such a nice place."

Mama, who had come downstairs to their apartment to get ready for work, scoffed when Aunt Teri said that. "I don't think wealth makes you immune to danger."

"Well, has he attacked in Beverly Hills?" Aunt Teri replied, folding her arms in front of her chest. "No, he has not. He wouldn't dare. Not with all those movie stars."

Bug told Aunt Teri that the Midnight Marauder had attacked Burbank, which according to Beth Ann, was lousy with movie stars.

"Burbank is not Beverly Hills," Aunt Teri sniffed.

Bug couldn't argue with that. "Can Frankie come?"

Aunt Teri frowned, looking as if she was sucking on a lemon. Mama answered for her. "Of course Frankie can come." Teri started to object, but Mama cut her off. "It's why you're here. To look after the children."

"That child is not my family," Aunt Teri said.

"He's our family," Mama said, "and while you're here, he's yours, too."

She shot Teri one of her looks. Aunt Teri's sigh was as gusty as the Santa Ana winds, but she backed down. "Fine. Frankie can come."

When Bug told Frankie the news, he said he didn't want to go.

"Why not?" Bug asked.

"Looking at houses. That sounds boring. We're supposed to be investigating."

"I know," Bug agreed. "But maybe it won't be boring. One house has a harem."

"What's that?" Frankie asked.

"I'm not sure," Bug admitted. "Please come. We can find out together."

"Your aunt doesn't like me," Frankie said.

"She doesn't like anyone," Bug said. "That's just how she is."

"And you're sure she doesn't know about me?"

"I'm sure."

Just then Danny emerged, yawning, up two hours earlier than normal because that was when the real surfers went. "I'm going to the beach today if you want to tag along."

"I have to go with Aunt Teri on a Lifestyles of the Rich and Famous tour," Bug said sullenly.

"What about you?" Danny asked Frankie.

Frankie didn't have to go with Aunt Teri. She was not technically in charge of him, and Bug knew her aunt would not object if Frankie went to the beach. If she were Frankie, she'd sure rather go to the beach than spend the day on a boring bus. "You go on without me," she told Frankie.

But it was as if Frankie, without ever having been told, understood rule number four—always stay together.

"Nope," he said. "I want to see a harem."

Mama had arranged for Aunt Teri to borrow Phillip's car, but she refused to drive it. So she took Mama's instead. She was nervous about traffic, so she made Frankie and Bug leave so early they got to Beverly Hills at nine thirty in the morning, a full hour and a half before the tour began.

The streets were quiet, most of the stores were still closed, but Aunt Teri said they'd window-shop. "Let's play a game," she said. "In each store, pick out which outfit you like best." She pointed to a display of poofy dresses with curlicue collars. "Which one would you wear?"

Bug and Frankie exchanged a quick look. Was she asking both of them?

"I'd wear that one," Teri said, pointing to the frilliest one in the center, blue with shiny sequins on the hem. She turned to Bug. "What about you?"

"I don't like to wear dresses," Bug replied.

Aunt Teri sighed. "You'll grow out of your tomboy phase one of these days." She turned to Frankie, and Bug's heart thundered in her chest as she imagined her aunt saying the same thing to him. But instead all she said was, "Her mother was like that when she was younger too."

"She was?" Bug asked, perking up.

"Oh yes. Co was always running around in the fields, making friends with the farmhands like a wild child." She clucked her tongue. "On second thought, maybe she didn't grow out of it."

"Mama wears dresses all the time," Bug protested, but Aunt Teri didn't answer. Instead she carried on her window-shopping game. She had all kinds of opinions on the clothes. Which were trashy, which were classy.

"We could be investigating," Frankie whispered after they'd been doing this a while. "I got a new notebook." He pulled out the kind of composition notebook Bug used for school. On the cover he'd written: *Trip Diary*. "It's a decoy," Frankie explained. "So no one finds out what we're doing."

"Smart! Should we write down leads like we did for the Midnight Marauder?" Bug asked.

Frankie nodded.

"Four hundred dollars for a skirt?" Aunt Teri was asking. "Is it made of gold?"

"Aunt Teri," Bug said. "We're a little tired. Can we sit on a bench and wait for you?"

"Fine," Aunt Teri said. "But stay in the shade. You don't want to wind up all dark like your brother."

"What did she mean about staying in the shade?" Frankie asked after they'd sat down.

"She doesn't want me to get too tan, otherwise I'll look Salvadoran, like Danny does." Bug paused. "Like my father was."

"What's wrong with looking Salvadoran?" Frankie asked.

"Some people don't like Salvadorans," Bug explained. "Or

Mexicans. Or people like that. And I guess Aunt Teri is one of them."

"But aren't *you* half Salvadoran?" Frankie asked.

Bug nodded.

Frankie was silent for a long while, nodding slowly to himself. Then he turned to Bug and said, "So you get it?"

"Get what?"

The composition book sat on Frankie's lap, but he didn't open it. He just thumbed at the cover, as if he was thinking. And then he put his hand on top of Bug's the way Mama sometimes did to make her feel better. It was the biggest display of affection she'd ever seen from Frankie.

"What it's like for people to be mad at you," Frankie said, "just for being you."

"Welcome to the Lifestyles of Wealthy Celebrities tour," the guide began after they'd climbed onto the bus, "which is not affiliated with the television show *Lifestyles of the Rich and Famous*."

The bus was a double-decker, and when she'd seen it, Bug had been excited—she'd never been on a two-story one before—but when they boarded, Aunt Teri had made them sit downstairs, and though she didn't say so, Bug knew it was to keep her out of the sun. This, coupled with what Frankie had said, left Bug's stomach in knots.

She knew Aunt Teri loved her. She said so in the birthday cards she sent, always with a crisp five-dollar bill tucked inside. But was it possible her aunt didn't like her? And was this how it was for Frankie at home?

As the bus chugged through the leafy streets of Beverly Hills, Aunt Teri oohed and aahed and snapped picture after picture. "It is beyond me why your mother moved to Los Angeles and didn't choose to settle someplace like this."

Bug avoided stating the obvious: because they weren't rich. Or famous.

"Your mother was so beautiful," Aunt Teri said. "Prettiest girl in town. Prettier than any Hollywood actress. She was home-coming queen. She could've had the pick of the litter. Married someone respectable. Lived in a mansion like this." She gestured to a large ivy-covered brick house behind a tall row of hedges. "Instead she threw it all away. On someone like that." Aunt Teri gestured to one of the men trimming the hedges.

"A gardener?" Frankie asked.

"A farmhand," Aunt Teri said.

"My father was a teacher," Bug said.

"Well, he spent all his time among the farmworkers, so he might as well have been one," Aunt Teri replied. "He smelled like one, that's for sure."

Bug swallowed the urge to defend her father's smell, which, for all she knew, was the best smell in the world. But she wanted Aunt Teri to keep going, to tell her things about her father. So she tried Mama's trick and kept her mouth shut so Teri would keep talking. And it worked.

"Your mother was always so naive, always trying to save the world." Aunt Teri frowned, like saving the world was a bad thing. "He must have seen her from a mile away. Picked her up easy as a . . ." Aunt Teri paused to consider it. "A grape!" Then she laughed.

"A grape?" Bug asked, not getting the joke.

"Oh, they met when the grape pickers were striking. Such rabble-rousers. It's one thing for Co, but your father, he was a guest in our country. You'd think that he'd be grateful." She turned toward the window. "Oh, would you look at that house? Isn't it a beauty?"

"It's nice," Bug said without looking. "What did my grandparents think of my father?" she asked casually, as if this was not forbidden territory.

"Oh, they hated him," Aunt Teri replied almost merrily. "That's why your mother had to keep him secret."

Mama had kept her father a secret? Why?

"Of course *I* knew," Aunt Teri bragged. "Co could never keep anything from me. We were very close."

Bug had a hard time picturing that. "Did they ever find out?" she asked. But then she realized this was a dumb question. Of course they'd found out! After all, Mama had Danny and Bug.

"Oh, you bet. And were there ever fireworks. They kicked your mother right out of the house."

When Bug gasped, Aunt Teri put her hand over her mouth, as if realizing she'd said too much. "How many bathrooms did you say were in that house?" she asked the tour guide.

"Eleven," he said.

"Why did they kick Mama out?"

"Eleven," she repeated. "Wouldn't you love to live in a place like that?"

Bug thought about their apartment, with her not-really-a-bedroom bedroom and only one bathroom that Danny was always hogging. But upstairs was Phillip, and downstairs was Hedvig. And inside were Mama and Danny. All people who loved Bug and liked Bug, and who would never turn her away, no matter what she did.

She wouldn't trade that for all the bathrooms in the world.

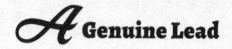A Genuine Lead

MAMA CAME HOME THAT NIGHT with a bag of fish and chips and some good news.

"Phillip is being discharged in the morning."

"Hooray!" Bug said, dousing her French fries with vinegar, which made them deliciously mushy and pungent.

"I'll go get him in the morning and take the day off," Mama continued. "Phillip will stay here with us for the first few days, along with Frankie." Mama turned to Aunt Teri. "You can shift up to his place."

"I most certainly will not!"

"You'd have the apartment all to yourself," Mama replied. "Bug, ease up on the vinegar."

"I won't stay there. Lord knows what I'll catch."

"It's really clean up there," Bug said. "Way cleaner than here."

"There is a kind of filth you can't see," Aunt Teri said.

"You mean like the words coming out of your mouth?" Mama countered, her voice rising, which it almost never did. Bug wasn't clear what they were fighting about. Phillip's place was immaculate—everyone knew that, even if Teri didn't believe it.

Mama took three breaths, in, out, something she did a lot when Teri visited.

"Phillip can't handle too many steps, and he needs someone to look after him," she said, her voice calmer. "You are welcome to stay down here, but you'll be sharing the couch with me."

Bug dipped her fry into a puddle of vinegar and popped it in her mouth.

"I'd sooner sleep on a box in the street than sleep in that man's apartment." She sniffed. "If you ask me, he deserved what he got."

"Why would Phillip deserve it?" Bug asked as Frankie kicked her under the table.

"He doesn't. Nobody does," Mama replied before turning to Teri. "What a despicable thing to say!"

"Well, it's true. How can you look at this plague and not see it as God's punishment?"

"What plague? What punishment?" Bug asked, and Frankie kicked her again.

"Nothing, sweetie," Mama said, turning to Teri. "That's not how *my* God operates. And while you're a guest in my home, I'd ask you to keep such hateful opinions to yourself."

"A guest you begged to come help you with these children, in case you've forgotten!" Aunt Teri reminded her.

"Like you'd let me forget it," Mama grumbled.

Frankie and Bug looked at each other. Mama and Aunt Teri looked less like grown-ups than siblings who were about to get into a punch-up.

And they might have, had Danny not barged through the door. "Sorry I'm late. Fish and chips! Yum! I'm starving."

No one spoke as Danny sat down and loaded his plate with fish and French fries and tartar sauce. "How was the rich-people tour?" he asked Bug.

"Oh yes," Mama said, her voice chirpy and bright. "Did you see any movie stars?" She sounded so interested, and if you didn't know any better, you'd think she was genuinely curious. But Bug knew Mama didn't give two flips about movie stars. "They're just people," she'd often said in the blasé tone of someone who regularly saw famous TV reporters like Tad

Draper, not to mention the mayor, who was always on TV.

"No, but we saw some gorgeous homes," Aunt Teri said. "It seems so nice in Beverly Hills, and safe." She split a French fry in two and ate half. "I'd love to see you and the kids settled there. The guide told me the schools are excellent."

"We go to a good school," Bug interjected, before she remembered that Danny wouldn't be going there this fall. "I mean I do."

"Yes. And that terrible commute. If you lived in Visalia, you could ride your bike to school. Doesn't that sound nice?"

"So do you want us to move to Beverly Hills or Visalia?" Mama asked.

"I'm just trying to be helpful. I don't see why you always make it so hard on yourself."

"Life's hard, Teri. Haven't you heard?"

"Indeed," Aunt Teri said. "But you always seem to look for extra helpings."

They continued the meal in silence. When they were finished, Frankie offered to do the dishes.

"It's Danny's night," Bug protested.

"That's okay," Frankie said. "You'll help me."

Bug was about to protest again, but then Frankie kicked her underneath the table a third time and raised his eyebrows, which

Bug knew meant he had something important to tell her. "Fine, I'll help."

"Thanks," Danny said, reaching for the telephone. "I can go and meet Whitney."

"You just got back," Teri said. "And it's a little late for going out."

"It's not even eight," Danny protested.

"Go on," Mama said. "Just stay where it's well-lit and full of people."

"You do let your children run wild, Co," Teri said. "No wonder."

In the kitchen, Bug turned on the taps. Frankie clanged the dishes extra loud.

"What is it?" Bug asked. "It better be good to let Danny out of dishes."

"That thing your aunt said about Phillip deserving what he got," Frankie said. "It's a clue."

"What do you mean?"

"I'm guessing she knows he's gay."

"He is?" Bug asked, confused. "He's nice and all but not exactly the jolliest person. And anyway, why would that bother Aunt Teri?"

"Not happy gay," Frankie whispered. "Homosexual gay."

"What's that?"

"It means, he doesn't like girls romantically; he likes boys."

"What?" Bug said. "Since when?"

"Since always." Frankie paused. "Didn't you know?"

Was it possible to know something and not know it at the same time? This was the first time anyone had told her Phillip was gay, the first time anyone had explained what gay was, but hadn't she known Phillip was a little different? A good kind of different, but still different.

"Why didn't anyone tell me?" Bug asked, stung because yet another important thing had been concealed from her. "Does Danny know? Hedvig?"

"I don't know."

"Is it a secret?"

Frankie scrubbed a smear of ketchup off a plate as he considered it. "Sort of."

"Why?"

"Because of how people will react."

"You mean like Aunt Teri?"

Frankie nodded. "He teaches kids to play piano, and if the parents find out, they might not let him near their kids." Frankie rinsed a plate and handed it to Bug to dry.

"Why?"

"People don't like gay people."

"Why?"

"I dunno. I guess they think being gay is wrong."

"Well, that's dumb," Bug said, stacking the plates back in the cupboard. "And I still don't get how it's a clue."

"Think about it: Why would they say Phillip was mugged, if his wallet wasn't stolen?"

Bug didn't get it. And then, suddenly, she did. Why Aunt Teri wouldn't stay in his apartment or drive his car. Her thinking Phillip "deserved" what happened to him. "You think Phillip was beat up because . . . ?" Bug began.

"He's gay?" Frankie finished. "I do." He bowed his head and his body curled into the familiar slump. "I wish I didn't, but I do."

Zeus

IT TOOK MAMA AND DANNY ten minutes to help Phillip get up one flight of stairs. When Bug saw him, she almost cried. Not just because he looked terrible. Bug now knew that Phillip was fifty-five, but this was the first time he seemed old to her. And it scared her.

As if he could read her thoughts, Phillip teased, "I don't look *that* bad, do I?"

"Y-you look great," Bug stammered.

"One of the dearest things about you, Beatrice, is that you're a terrible liar."

Was she? She'd been investigating the Midnight Marauder all summer and hadn't told him, or Mama. And she now knew

Phillip was gay, and what gay meant, but hadn't told anyone. Did that make her a liar? Or a secret-keeper?

"Do you want anything?" Frankie asked Phillip.

"I wouldn't mind an ice pack." And then, pulling out a five-dollar bill, Phillip added, "And how about Daniel goes to get us some donuts."

"Sure." Danny took the money and left. Bug hopped up and went to the fridge and got both the ice and the pitcher of lemonade she'd squeezed that morning. She made a great show of pouring a glass and handing it to Phillip, who hesitated and then took a sip and winced.

Lemons, Bug realized, were awful for cuts. "You don't have to drink that," she said.

"But I want to. You've mastered the recipe." Phillip looked around. "Where's Santa Theresa?"

"She went out," Mama said.

"In this crime-ridden ghetto?" Phillip shook his head.

"She took Mama's car to Beverly Hills," Bug said. "She's going on another fancy house tour."

Frankie and Bug had been invited along, but they had said no because Frankie wanted to be home when Phillip arrived. But they'd agreed to do whatever boring thing Teri suggested tomorrow to see if they could get any more information out of her.

"You two don't need to hover over me all day," Phillip said, grimacing at Mama. "I have Colleen for that."

"Indeed you do," Mama said, laying a hand on Phillip's shoulder.

Danny returned with the donuts. He'd gotten glazed jellies, which were Bug's favorites, and Boston creams, which were Frankie's and Mama's.

Danny, licking the chocolate glaze off his fingers, casually asked Phillip, "Do they have any suspects in your case?"

"Not as of yet," Phillip replied.

"Did you look at a police lineup?" Danny asked.

"Not yet," Phillip said.

"Do the police have any leads?" Danny asked.

Frankie and Bug looked at each other. Neither had told Danny about the new investigation. Was he doing one of his own?

"Not many," Phillip replied.

"Can you ask the mayor to help?" Danny asked Mama.

Mama and Phillip exchanged a look. "I'm sure the mayor has bigger fish to fry right now," Phillip said. "What with the Midnight Marauder still at large."

"And how do you know for sure this wasn't the Midnight

Marauder?" Danny asked. "I mean, you were attacked at night. Not far from here."

Bug and Frankie exchanged a look. Phillip had been attacked nearby. That was new information—and it made no sense. He was meant to have been away for the night. Mama and Phillip exchanged another look. "We just know," Phillip said.

At noon, Phillip shooed them all away, and Mama told Danny to take them to the beach. Though it was hot—and would stay hot until Halloween—Bug could feel autumn's breath on her neck. Bug had heard people say that Southern California had no seasons, but she begged to differ. Maybe there were no crisp fall days, no snow, but the seasons at the beach distinguished themselves just as surely as they did anywhere. Maybe not in temperatures, but by the shorter lines at the food stands, the empty spaces on the sand. The crowds were thinning.

At Muscle Beach, Frankie and Bug sat on their bench under the palm tree. As Bug watched an airplane take off over the water, her melancholy deepened. Unless she could convince Mama and Phillip he should stay, Frankie would soon be on such a plane. Before Phillip got hurt, this was going to be hard enough. But now that he was out of commission, Mama said, for at least a month, it was even more complicated.

But what if they really did it? Found Phillip's attacker? Then they'd be heroes. Maybe not big enough heroes to get lifetime passes to Disneyland, but big enough for Frankie to be allowed to stay. "We have to find out who did this to Phillip!" she said fervently.

"I know," Frankie agreed. "That's what we're doing."

"But we should do more."

"Like what?"

"I don't know. Looking for leads."

"How?"

On the detective shows, they asked everyone in the area questions. Why were they just relying on Aunt Teri? Bug looked around. In the distance, she saw Zeus skating down the board-walk. "I have an idea," she said, grabbing Frankie's hand and calling to Danny that they'd be right back.

They caught up with Zeus in front of Sidewalk Café, where he was doing a dance routine to "Walk Like an Egyptian" for the patrons sitting at the outdoor tables. Bug waited impatiently for the song to end and for Zeus to see her.

"Bugsy!" he called.

"Hi, Zeus. Remember my friend Frankie?"

"'Course I do," Zeus said with a little twirl on his skates. "Bug and Frankie. Frankie and Bug."

Frankie and Bug. Bug remembered how she'd bristled at that. Now it sounded right, like peanut butter and jelly, two things that went together.

"Can we ask you some questions?" Bug asked.

"Ask and ye shall receive," Zeus replied with another twirl.

"We're investigating an attack," Frankie said.

"The Midnight Marauder has everyone aflutter." And then he started spinning again.

"We don't think it's the Midnight Marauder," Bug said. "It's a friend of ours, who's—" She stopped herself. She wasn't sure if she should tell even if she wasn't saying who it was.

"Gay," Frankie finished. "We think our friend got beat up because he's gay."

"The fearful fear what they do not know and become the thing the rest of us fear," Zeus said, holding his toe stopper in one hand as he extended his leg into a gliding arabesque in front of the impressed diners.

"What's he mean?" Bug whispered.

"I think that people are scared of Phillip," Frankie replied.

"Who'd be scared of Phillip?" Bug asked. But then she realized her own aunt was.

When Zeus returned to them, Bug asked, "Do you know anything about attacks on gay people?"

"Not for me to know. But go with the flow. Flow knows the way." And then Zeus picked up his tip hat, perched his boom box on his shoulder, and skated away.

"Well, that was a bust," Frankie said.

"I know. Let's go get ice cream. Maybe Bian will know something," she suggested.

But Bian did not know anything about it. She scooped Frankie and Bug their usual—caramel swirl and vanilla—but didn't charge them for it.

"I go back to school next week," Bian said. "Summer's ending."

Bug licked her ice cream. Not even the sweet caramel could take away the achy feeling inside her. "I know it is."

"Where have you been?" asked a frantic Danny when they returned to Muscle Beach. "You said you'd be right back. And that was an hour ago!"

Bug was surprised to see Danny so upset.

"We lost track of time," Frankie explained.

"We were about to send a posse out to look for you," Duane said. "Thought maybe the Midnight Marauder got wind of you poking around and did you in." He made a slicing gesture across his throat.

"We're not investigating the Midnight Marauder anymore," Frankie said. "We're investigating something else." He paused. "Or we're trying to."

"What?" Danny asked.

Frankie looked at Bug. Bug looked at Frankie.

"Phillip?" Danny guessed.

Frankie nodded. "He wasn't mugged. His wallet was right next to his bed at the hospital."

Danny knocked his temple with his knuckles. "You're right. I didn't even think about it when he took the money out for the donuts."

"Something's fishy," Bug said. "We were trying to get leads, talking to Zeus."

"Was he any help?"

"Not really," Bug replied.

"He said we should 'go with the flow,'" Frankie says. "'Flow knows the way.'"

"You know how he talks," Bug added.

"Go with the *flow*," Vanessa interjected. "I bet he means Florence."

"Florence?" Bug asked.

"Goes by Flo. Or Flo-Rida. Black, with the pink wig. Sometimes skates with Zeus."

Frankie's eyes went wide. "Flo's a person," he said. "*That* person?"

"That'd be my guess," Vanessa said.

"Do you know how we can reach Flo?" Bug asked.

"Sure do," Vanessa said. She pulled out a battered leather notebook from her gym bag and scribbled down an address on a piece of paper. "Here you go."

Bug stared at the slip. They were really doing it. Following leads. Like detectives. She turned to Danny. Tomorrow Mama would be back at work and would insist that Frankie and Bug stay with Aunt Teri. This was their day. Their shot.

"Can we go?" she begged.

Danny hesitated.

"Please," Frankie added.

"Flo's good people," Vanessa said. "They'll be fine."

Danny looked at Bug. "One hour," he said. "And don't tell Mom. Or Phillip."

Bug and Frankie were already racing away. "We won't if you won't," they called.

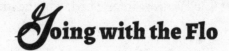

Going with the Flo

THE ADDRESS VANESSA HAD given them was for one of the junk shops on Abbot Kinney, which was where he worked. Or she. Bug wasn't sure which one to use. With Frankie it was easy, obvious. With Flo, less so.

"We'll just ask," Frankie said matter-of-factly when Bug expressed this concern.

"Isn't that rude?" Bug asked.

Frankie shrugged. "Ruder than calling someone the wrong thing?"

The clerk in the shop directed Frankie and Bug to the back, where Flo was going through a box of clothes. There was no spangled unitard, just jeans and a tank top. No hot-pink wig, just a smooth shaved brown head. But even without makeup and a wig, Flo was something to see.

"Y'all wanna take a picture? It'll last longer," Flo said in a raspy, amused voice.

"Sorry," Bug apologized, feeling dumb. She was accustomed to unusual people in Venice.

"Close your mouth, before you swallow a fly," Flo told Frankie, but it was said with a smile.

"I'm sorry," Frankie said.

"He's from Ohio," Bug explained.

"That right?" Flo laughed. "I'm from Tennessee."

Mama was from Visalia. Phillip and Frankie from Ohio. Bian from Vietnam. Was anyone in Venice from Venice?

"Are you a he or a she?" Bug blurted out when Frankie failed to ask the pressing question.

"That depends on the day," Flo replied breezily, shaking the dust out of a paisley dress. "So what can I help you two with?"

"We're investigating a crime," Frankie said.

"That so?" Flo said with a slight smile. "What kind of crime? Someone steal your roller skates?"

"Someone beat up my uncle," Frankie said.

Flo's smile disappeared.

"Who is gay," Frankie added.

Flo's mouth curled into a frown. "I'm very sorry to hear that."

"We're trying to figure out if he was beat up *because* he was gay," Bug explained.

"Why else would he be?" Flo replied.

"For money," Bug said. "Or because the person who beat him is a psychopath like the Midnight Marauder."

"If I hear one more word about the Midnight Marauder, I'm gonna maraud someone myself," Flo said with an exasperated sigh. "We're being beaten up left and right, but do you hear about that on the news? No, you don't."

Frankie and Bug looked at each other. Frankie's hunch *was* right.

"Who's being beat up?" Bug asked.

"All manner of queers, but the gay men getting it worst right now."

"Why?"

"Oh, folks don't need a reason. Old as time to beat on what you don't understand. But with AIDS, it's given them all a mission."

"AIDS?" Bug asked.

"The queer cancer. The gay plague." Flo looked disgusted.

Plague. That was what Aunt Teri had said.

"It's a disease killing our people. And if it weren't enough our own bodies are attacking us, we got actual people attacking us too." Flo's tone softened. "I'm sure your uncle will be fine."

"So do you think being gay is why he got beat up?" Bug pressed.

"I'd be surprised if it were any other reason. It's open season on queers."

"You keep saying 'queer,'" Frankie said. "Isn't that a bad thing?"

"In some circles, I suppose, but I mean it as a term of love for gays, lesbians, bisexuals, transsexuals." Flo tossed the quickest look at Frankie before adding, "You know, all us folk . . ."

At the *us folk*, Bug's breath caught. Did Flo know? Would Frankie be upset? She glanced over. Frankie didn't look upset. He had a funny little half smile on his lips. His eyes were open and shining.

"Is that what I am?" he asked in a quavering voice.

"It's not *what* you are, it's *who* you are. And that's up to you. But I know plenty like you who call themselves transsexual."

"*Transsexual*," Frankie repeated. "So there *is* a word for it."

"Oh, honey, there's a word for everything on God's green earth. And if there isn't, we can just make one up."

"And there are other people? Like me?" Frankie asked in a halting voice.

Flo laid a manicured hand on Frankie's shoulder. "Sweet boy. More than you could ever imagine."

After Flo sent them away with a business card and a phone number, Frankie and Bug found Danny, and the three of them went to Tower 19. The water was unusually calm, in contrast to the thoughts crashing around in Bug's mind. There was a plague killing gay people. How did you get it? Did only gay people get it? Did Phillip have it? Was this why Teri was so scared of him? Should Bug be scared of him too? *Could* she be scared of Phillip? She didn't think so. It would be like being scared of Danny, or Mama.

As riled up as Bug was, Frankie seemed serene, as if the meeting with Flo had answered a question instead of raising a zillion new ones. He lay on his back, floating, staring at the clouds, in a world of his own. And when they got out of the water, he lay down in the sun and fell asleep.

Bug contemplated all the questions while watching Danny, who was sitting on a surfboard in the water, along with a girl who had corkscrew curls and sun-burnished skin. After a while, Danny slid off her board and swam back to shore.

"Is that Whitney?" Bug asked. "She's pretty."

Danny flushed. "She's a really good surfer." He tugged at the zipper of his wet suit.

"Did you know about AIDS?"

"Uh-huh," Danny replied.

"Does Phillip have it?" Bug asked.

"Why would Phillip have it?" Danny replied, pulling the zipper the rest of the way down, revealing his newly chiseled chest.

"Because, you know . . ."

"Because he's gay," Danny said matter-of-factly, as he shimmied his arms out of the wet suit.

"You knew? Who told you?"

"No one told me. I just figured it out. Hold the towel, will you?"

Bug held the towel around his waist like a curtain while Danny continued to change. "Do you also know about . . . ?" She trailed off. She meant to say *Frankie* but realized it wasn't her place to ask.

"Frankie?" Danny answered for her, kicking off the wet suit. "Yeah. He told me after he told you."

"Oh," Bug paused to hand Danny his swim trunks. "So do you think Phillip might have got beat up because he was gay?"

Danny nodded slowly. "Yeah, I do."

"Because he has AIDS?"

"Phillip does *not* have AIDS!"

"But he's gay," Bug said.

"So?" Danny asked, taking the towel from Bug and slinging it around his neck.

"Gay people get AIDS."

"*Some* gay people get AIDS," Danny said. "But other people do too. Like that kid Ryan White, who got it from a blood transfusion. Remember we saw that TV program about him?"

Bug remembered. He was a boy not much older than her who'd been on TV with Elizabeth Taylor, the beautiful actress who had been married like seven times. She didn't really understand what the show had been about. She remembered watching him and Elizabeth Taylor and feeling a little jealous because he was friends with a movie star. Now that she knew it was because he had a deadly disease, she felt a little bad about that.

When Frankie woke up, the back of his legs sunburned, they packed up and walked toward home. Danny went on ahead with Whitney, with Bug and Frankie lingering behind.

"Are they boyfriend and girlfriend?" Frankie asked.

Bug wasn't sure. They weren't kissing or even holding hands, but they kept bumping shoulders in a way that Bug recognized was more than friendly.

"I can't imagine Danny having a girlfriend," Bug said. "He's just Danny."

"How come you call him that?"

"What?"

"Danny. Everyone else calls him Daniel."

"Well, everyone else calls me Bug, but Phillip calls me Beatrice."

"Do you *want* to be called one or the other?" Frankie asked.

Bug had never really thought about it. Bug was her name, it was how she thought of herself. But she liked that Phillip called her Beatrice, like it was a special nickname. "I like both."

"Does your brother like both?" Frankie asked.

"He doesn't care." But then she stopped. Because hadn't Danny expressly asked to be called Daniel? Hadn't he corrected her a bunch of times when she'd used the wrong name? She'd told herself she was calling him *Danny* out of habit, but she now realized there was more to it. Danny was her brother. Daniel was the person who'd left her behind.

When they got home, Frankie went up to Phillip's to change. Danny lingered on the sidewalk with Whitney. To give him space, Bug went inside and waited for him in front of their apartment door.

"You locked out?" he asked when he came upstairs and saw Bug standing there.

"No. I just wanted to thank you, Daniel," she said.

The name felt strange on her tongue, but also familiar. It was her father's name, after all.

"For what?" he asked, hanging up his towel on the pegs Mama installed in the hall to keep them from tracking sand into the apartment.

"For today, Daniel." She knew it would take practice to call Danny "Daniel," but she wanted him to know she would try.

If he was surprised or happy to hear her use this name, he didn't show it. He opened the door, and then he and Bug went through it, together.

he Price Is Right

"HOW WAS EVERYBODY'S DAY?" Aunt Teri asked that night as they ate takeout from the Chinese Diner. She was in jolly spirits, having snapped a photo of Cher, or someone she was 98 percent sure was Cher, outside her home in the Hollywood Hills. She'd dropped off the film at the kiosk in front of the Sav-On Drugs, splurging for the twenty-four-hour processing so she could get prints back and have proof.

Speaking of proof, Frankie and Bug were now certain that Phillip had been beaten up because he was gay, but they needed proof.

"Our day was fine. Nothing special," Danny said, giving Bug and Frankie a conspiratorial look.

"Yes, fine," Bug repeated.

"Fine and fine," Phillip replied.

"What about you?" Frankie asked Phillip. "How are you feeling?"

"Never better," Phillip quipped.

Bug could tell by the furrow between his brows that this was not true.

"Well," Aunt Teri continued merrily, "I had a wonderful day. The tour guide was fantastic. He was a game show regular. Did you know there was such a thing? He's been on *The Price Is Right*, *The Joker's Wild*, and *Match Game*. He won a washing machine, a camper, and eleven hundred dollars!"

"Is that so?" Mama asked.

"It is. And he told me how to get tickets to be in the television audience and maybe get picked for *The Price Is Right*. It's so easy, I had no idea. All you have to do is wait in line. I'm going to try tomorrow. Apparently, they accept children as young as eight in the audience, so you can come," she said to Bug. She must have been feeling pretty generous, because, without prodding, she turned to Frankie and added, "And you, too."

"Thank you," Bug mumbled, even though being in a studio audience of a show where people had to guess the price of washing machines sounded like the most boring thing she could imagine.

"Maybe I'll win a car," Aunt Teri said. "Maybe even a convertible. I used to have a 1968 cherry-red Mustang convertible."

Bug and Danny exchanged a look. Not the car again! Mama put a hand over Teri's. "We know you did," she said.

Aunt Teri paused and forced a little smile at Mama before turning to Bug. "We'll have to get an early start to wait in line. That's how you get in. So if we get there by seven, when the doors open at ten we'll be right at the front."

Correction: *this* sounded like the most boring thing she could imagine.

"We have to wake up at six to go wait in a line for three hours?" Bug asked.

"Wake up at five," Teri responded. "We'll leave at six. To beat the traffic."

"But there's no traffic that early." The protest died on Bug's lips. The deal, *her* deal, was that they went where Teri went and in return Frankie got to stay.

"I think it's okay if the kids want to sit this one out," Phillip said. "I'm feeling better."

He didn't look better. His face was like a bad Crayola mash-up, black and blue under his eyes, and yellow and green on his cheeks.

His knuckles were all scraped up. He still had trouble climbing the stairs.

"I thought I came here to take care of the children while he recuperated," Aunt Teri said to Mama, not even looking at Phillip.

"We'll go with Aunt Teri," Bug said. She shot Frankie a look, and he nodded. Bug knew he didn't really want to go, same as her. But Phillip needed rest, and they needed proof.

"And Aunt Teri is our best source," she whispered to Frankie as they scraped the leftover kung pao chicken off the dishes in the kitchen.

"Source for what?"

"Information," Bug said. "Phillip won't tell us where he was Friday night. And even if Mama knows, she definitely won't tell. She's very good at keeping a poker face. But Aunt Teri lets things slip all over the place. She gave us our first lead. Who knows what information she might have?"

As it turned out, there were lots of people whose idea of a good time was to wake up at the crack of dawn and wait in line outside the studio, which was in a place called Television City that sounded way cooler than it was. The line was already snaking around the building when they got there. Aunt Teri frowned, and when she saw all the people—many wearing T-shirts with decals on them, or special outfits—she frowned harder. "We should've dressed up so that Johnny Olson would tell us to 'Come on down,'" she said.

"Maybe you should come back tomorrow," Bug said, regretting agreeing to this. Three hours waiting in line was three of Hedvig's soap operas, and a whole lot more boring. Which was saying something.

"Oh, no. We're here now. And maybe having you two with me will help me stand out, so make sure you smile a lot," she said, laying out a blanket on the sidewalk, the one, Bug noted, Mama normally slung over them while they watched TV in winter. Then she presented Bug with a large floppy bonnet. "Put this on so you don't get too dark."

"I don't think Johnny Olson will care," Bug said crossly. She did not like hats. They made her ears itch.

"Oh, you'd be surprised," Aunt Teri said. "Everyone cares. It's a blessing you take after your mother and not your father."

"That's a mean thing to say!" Bug cried, even though she had felt, at least with the skinheads, this might be a little bit true. She glanced at Frankie, who was staring at her with wide eyes. He nodded slightly, as if to say, *You tell her.*

"You might not like Salvadorans," Bug continued. "But my father is one, and you shouldn't talk about him like that."

"Are you calling me prejudiced?" Aunt Teri huffed. "I have a friend who's from Mexico. Just ask her if I'm prejudiced."

"But you don't want me to look like my father. And you said Mama should've married someone else and not some"—Bug paused to remember the term—"rabble-rouser."

"Well, he was a rabble-rouser. Getting the pickers to strike. Causing all manner of headaches. With the farmers, and for your mother." She sighed. "But I have nothing against him personally."

"Then why don't you want me to look like him?"

"Because it'll be easier for you."

"Easier how?"

"People will treat you differently if they think you're foreign."

"What people?" Bug asked.

"All people. You'd be surprised." Aunt Teri paused. "Even your own family."

For a moment, Bug thought Aunt Teri was referring to herself, but then she realized it was other family she was talking about, the ones Mama never spoke of. "You mean my grandparents?"

Aunt Teri sucked in her breath. "So you know?"

Bug felt a tingle go up her spine. She forced herself to stay calm, to have a poker face. "Of course I know," Bug fibbed. "Mama cried all the way down on the Greyhound."

As she said the words, Bug wondered, for the first time, *why* Mama had been crying on that bus. It wasn't like her father had just died. And why was she traveling alone, with a little boy and a new baby, to a town where she didn't know anyone, didn't have any place to go? She'd had to ask a stranger where the best place to live was. And why did she talk to Aunt Teri but not her own parents? And what did Hedvig mean when she told Mama that she also knew what it was like to be a refugee? Bug had been puzzled by that ever since the trip to Disneyland. According to the dictionary, *refugee* was a person who fled a foreign country to escape danger. She understood how Hedvig was a refugee, but how was Mama one?

"Who wouldn't cry after all that?" Teri replied.

All that. What all that? Bug needed to find out. And she needed to play her cards right. "Because my grandparents . . ." Bug trailed off, doing that trick Mama did to let other people fill in the blank.

"Offered her a deal with the devil," Teri said. Bug's heart throbbed in her chest, but she said nothing.

"Remind me of the deal," she said, forcing her voice to stay calm, to make it seem like she'd just forgotten this minor detail. And for a second, it seemed like it worked, because Aunt Teri opened her mouth, but then she snapped it shut, narrowing her eyes at Bug. "You'll have to discuss that with your mother," she said in a tight voice. Bug wanted to probe further, but when Aunt Teri added, "I wonder if they'll ship washing machines," Bug understood the conversation was over.

Things You Don't Want to Know

THE *PRICE IS RIGHT* TAPING took two hours, and though they got home at lunchtime, it felt like they'd been away for days. When Bug looked around her apartment, it seemed oddly unfamiliar, like someone had changed the paint colors a few shades.

"I'm taking a nap," Aunt Teri said. She had not been called to come on down, so she didn't win a new car or a washing machine or a trip to Hawaii. She took off her shoes and lay down on the couch.

"I'm going upstairs," Frankie announced.

After Frankie left and Aunt Teri fell asleep, Bug was alone, all the questions itching inside her like a swarm of mosquitoes biting her brain. What exactly did Aunt Teri mean, that people would treat you differently if you were foreign? Had Bug's own grandparents treated her differently? What deal with the devil had they offered Mama? Bug knew this was somehow related to the reason she never saw them, and maybe even the reason Mama left Visalia on that Greyhound, crying all the way to L.A.

She went to the bookcase and pulled down the photo album from the high shelf, thumbing through the familiar pictures until she got to the last one, of herself as a baby in Mama's arms, Danny the protective brother, Aunt Teri in the corner. Who, Bug now wondered, had taken that picture? Who was on the other side of the camera?

Bug knew Mama's rules and she knew Aunt Teri's rules, and under both sets, she was not allowed to go to the beach herself. But she needed answers. And at the moment, that was more important than any contract.

She found Danny at Muscle Beach, doing crunches as Whitney pressed on his feet. "Hey, Bug," he said breathlessly as he sat up. "What are you doing here?" He went back down and came back up. "I thought you were at *The Price Is Right*."

Sometimes when Bug was swimming, a giant wave would sneak up out of nowhere and wallop her. And that was what it felt like now as a tsunami of feelings crashed over her. Suddenly, she wasn't just crying, she was erupting with salty oceanic tears.

"Sweetie, what's wrong?" Whitney asked.

Danny jumped to his feet. "What happened?" he asked, real panic in his voice.

Bug didn't know how to explain what was wrong. And even if she could, she was sobbing too hard to speak.

Soon, all of Muscle Beach seemed to surround her. Randy and Duane and Bill and Vanessa and other people she didn't know. "Who hurt you?" Duane asked. "We'll hurt them worse."

"Was it the Midnight Marauder?" Randy asked, hopping from foot to foot.

"She doesn't look hurt," Vanessa said, inspecting Bug's face.

"And they say on the news the Midnight Marauder's hiding," Randy added. "No new killings in ten days."

All these people circling her, worried about her, made Bug feel warm and good and protected. Which somehow made her sob even harder.

"C'mon," Danny said, putting his towel around Bug's shoulders like a blanket. He led her out of Muscle Beach and to the drinking fountains, dabbing the towel's hem in the water and wiping her face, taking care of her like the protective big brother he'd always been.

When Bug's sobs had subsided to hiccupy gasps, Danny knelt in front of her, putting his hands on her shoulders. "What happened?"

"Why did Mama leave Visalia? Why did we move here? Why did she cry all the way down on the bus? Why do we see Aunt Teri but not our grandparents? What's a deal with the devil?" The questions came out in a whoosh, as if they'd been stuck up in her for a long time.

Danny did not have Mama's poker face. His chin wobbled and his cheeks went pink, so when he said, "I don't know," Bug knew it was a lie.

"Yes, you do!" Bug fired back. "Tell me!"

Danny paused to wipe the sweat on his brow away with his fuzzy wristband. "What did Teri tell you?"

"Nothing," Bug said.

"She must have told you something."

"She said people treat you differently if look, you know, foreign." She stopped, wondering if this would insult Danny, but he didn't look upset, at least not at her. "And she asked me if I knew why we'd come to Venice in the first place, and when I said I didn't, she said to ask Mama."

Danny nodded solemnly. "She's right. You should."

"But *you* know! And Teri knows." Bug paused. "Does Phillip know?"

"He's Mom's best friend," Danny answered in a gentle tone. "Of course he knows."

"Why does everyone know important things but me?" Bug cried out. "No one told me about Frankie or Phillip, which was bad enough. But this is about *me*." She jabbed herself possessively on the chest. "I have a right to know! I'm not a baby!"

With the tearstains on her face, Bug would not have been surprised if Danny had contradicted this. But instead he said, "I know you're not. But trust me, there are some things you don't want to know."

"But *you* know!" Bug said. "Mama told you!"

Danny nodded. "But only recently."

"When?"

"Around my birthday."

His birthday was in March, around the time, Bug now recalled, that Danny suddenly started needing space, asking to be called Daniel, calling himself Salvadoran, and learning Spanish.

"What did she tell you?"

Danny shook his head. "I'm not trying to be a jerk, Bug. But this is something you have to ask Mom. And when you do, if you need to talk about it, come find me. I'm here."

And then Danny did something he had not done in ages. He hugged her. And in her ear, he whispered, "I'll always be here."

Back at home, Frankie was waiting on the landing in front of Bug's apartment. "I need to talk to you," he hissed urgently.

Bug opened the door, bracing against Teri's scolding, but she was still snoring away on the couch. Bug led Frankie into Mama's room and locked the door behind them. She could hardly breathe. Her insides were full of so many feelings it was like there wasn't room for air.

"I found proof." Frankie held out an onionskin piece of paper in front of Bug. "Phillip keeps all his receipts in a folder. I went through them when he was sleeping."

"Oh," Bug said, a weird, icky feeling shuddering over her. She knew snooping like this was something detectives did, but with Phillip, it felt like spying.

"This is a receipt from the day the attack happened," Frankie whispered.

Bug looked at the paper. It was from a place called Roosterfish.

It was for twenty-seven dollars: twenty-two dollars plus a five-dollar tip. "A restaurant?"

Frankie nodded. "I think so. And I looked it up in the Yellow Pages. It's on Abbot Kinney."

"That's in Venice," Bug whispered.

"I know," Frankie said. "I looked it up on the map, too."

"Would someone attack Phillip at a restaurant for being gay?" Bug asked.

"I don't know," Frankie replied. "But I know who might."

Flo answered the phone on the sixth ring with a rushed "I told you I'm putting on my face and I'll get there when I get there," as if midway through a conversation with someone else.

Frankie and Bug, sharing the handset, paused, neither sure what to say.

"I'm hanging up now," Flo said.

"Wait," Frankie said.

"Who is this?" Flo asked.

"It's Frankie and Bug," Frankie replied. "We met you the other day at work. You said we could call if we had more questions."

"Well, hello, darlings. Lovely to hear from you, but I'm on

my way out the door, so I'll have to talk to you later."

"What's Roosterfish?" Bug blurted, not wanting to lose their opening.

Flo went silent for a minute and Bug thought the connection had ended. Until Flo said, "Why you want to know?"

"It's where my uncle was the night he got beat up."

The line went silent again. Then Flo said: "It's a gay bar." More silence. "I'm sorry." Even more silence. "I have to go now, but you two come see me tomorrow if you want to talk about this."

"Okay," Frankie said in a robotic voice.

After Flo hung up, they sat in more silence, the receiver off the hook until it started making the busy-signal sound. Bug gently put the phone back in the cradle while Frankie pulled out his leads book and wrote down the following.

Phillip was at a gay bar the night he was beaten up.

Phillip was beaten up for being gay.

He looked at Bug. "What kind of people would beat someone up outside a gay bar in Venice?" Bug asked, but as soon as the words were out, she knew the answer: The kind of people who attacked Japanese tourists. The kind of people who had come after Danny and called him that terrible name. The kind of scared people who became scary people.

Bug took the notebook and pen from Frankie. She paused, clicking and unclicking the tip of the ballpoint. She felt sick. It was one thing to chase after the Midnight Marauder. He was like a bogeyman, scary, but faraway. The skinheads were different. They lived here. They'd hassled her own brother, her own mother. Some of them went to Venice High School, where Danny would be starting in a few weeks. And they'd beaten up Phillip. She knew it was true because her Gut Voice was screaming that it was true. But oh, how she wished it weren't.

She wrote:

The skinheads attacked Phillip for being gay.

She handed the book to Frankie, hoping, this time, that he would laugh at her, tell her she was being crazy. Because then it wouldn't be true.

Frankie stared at the page for a long time, his face unreadable. Then he quietly closed the book and set it down. "I guess we solved the mystery." It should've been a triumph. Two kids solving a crime. But Frankie sounded so very sad, like he too understood that there were some things you just did not want to know.

*M*ama's Deal

NORMALLY BUG LOVED MEAT LOAF, or at least how Phillip made it, tangy with lots of onions that he fried until they turned crispy and sweet, with a topping made from bread crumbs and maple syrup. But the meat loaf Aunt Teri cooked that night for dinner tasted like sand.

Then again, tonight anything would've tasted like sand.

Mama chewed her own meat loaf a really long time. "Thanks for cooking, Teri," she said.

"Well, I thought someone around here ought to," Teri said.

Someone around here does cook. Phillip, Bug thought as she mashed the meat loaf with her fork, hoping it would make it look more eaten that way. Danny had stayed out with Whitney and Phillip was upstairs, so it was just her and Frankie and Mama stuck with Aunt Teri's meal.

"Don't play with your food," her aunt scolded.

Bug quickly ate a giant mouthful of meat loaf, chasing it down with a gulp of milk. Teri had put dinner on as soon as Mama got home, giving Bug no time to talk to her. She needed this meal to be over with so she could talk to Mama alone.

She managed a few more bites before scooping up some of the watery potatoes, which Aunt Teri had made from a box. (If he'd objected to concentrated lemonade, Bug could only imagine Phillip's horror at powdered potatoes.)

"Can I be excused?" Frankie asked. He'd eaten even less than Bug, pushing the food around his plate. "I want to go see Phillip."

"Of course," Mama said in a gentle voice. "I'll help Bug with dishes."

After Frankie left, Aunt Teri announced, "Now that the bathroom's free, I think I'll have a nice long soak." She went to the kitchen to get the Ajax to scrub out the tub.

"You're awful quiet tonight," Mama said as they cleared the dishes from the table. "Something on your mind?"

Bug nodded but didn't speak. There was too much on her

mind. And now that she was alone with Mama, she didn't know where to start. How to start.

Mama didn't push. They carried the dishes into the kitchen and filled the basin with soapy water, Mama washing, Bug drying. Mama was quiet, waiting for Bug to be ready.

It was now or never. She took a deep breath and on the exhale asked: "Why don't me and Danny ever go see our grandparents?"

Mama paused, midway through scrubbing the loaf pan. For a moment the only sound was of the dripping faucet. "Why do you ask?"

This was another of the tricks Mama used on reporters. Answer a question with a question. Bug was not falling for it.

"I know there's a reason. And I know Danny knows, and I want to know too."

Mama closed her eyes and took a deep breath. "What did Teri tell you?"

"She didn't tell me anything!" Bug cried. "Only that I should ask you why we don't see our grandparents."

"And this just came up out of nowhere?"

"Well, no. It sort of came up because she was telling me it's easier for me if I don't look Salvadoran like Danny does."

Mama squeezed the sponge so hard all the water came spurting out of it. "She shouldn't have said that."

"Why? I don't understand," Bug cried. "What happened? Why did we leave Visalia when I was a baby? Why did you cry all the way down on the Greyhound? Why are you a refugee? Why don't we know our grandparents? What deal with the devil?"

Mama replaced the sponge, dried her hands on the dish towel, and turned to Bug. "You're too young."

"I'm not too young!" Bug cried. "I know a lot. I know about Frankie." She paused before adding, "And Phillip, too."

Mama's eyebrows rose in surprise. "Oh?" she said.

"I know he's gay. And I also know there's a reason you left home and I know that you told Danny and then he started calling himself Daniel and needing space."

Mama's eyebrows rose again, which was how Bug knew she was right about this, too.

"I deserve to know. It's part of my life too, and it's not fair that you don't tell me."

For once, Mama didn't say life wasn't fair. Instead she let out a sigh that went on for a long time. "Look, you should know that I had problems with my parents well before I met your father."

"What do you mean?"

"We had different values. They were very against me being involved with the UFW."

"UFW?"

"It was a union, fighting for better farmworker conditions. I got involved in high school. They forbade me from participating, but I did it anyway. I just snuck out."

"Like you did with my father?"

Mama smiled at the memory. "Yes. That was how I met Daniel, and I knew my parents would not approve of him either, so I just kept sneaking."

"Why wouldn't they approve? Because he was Salvadoran?"

"Among other reasons."

"So they're prejudiced?" Bug asked.

"Everyone is prejudiced, Bug," Mama said. "It's what you do with the prejudice that matters."

"What do you mean?"

Mama shrugged. "You can either give in to the prejudice and treat people badly just because they're different from you. Or you can shine a light on it, to understand how arbitrary it all is and judge people for who they are, not what they are."

Bug thought about that. She knew which category Mama

was in—she wouldn't even hate the skinheads—but wasn't so sure about herself.

"So what happened when my grandparents found out about my father?" Bug asked.

"They kicked me out of the house and refused to speak to me."

"They did?" This was so dramatic. Like on *As the World Turns* when Lucinda Walsh found out about Lily and Holden. Was Lucinda prejudiced? Holden wasn't Salvadoran, but he was poor, and Lucinda and Lily were rich.

"They did. I thought they'd get over it, but they didn't. They refused to come to our wedding, or to Danny's christening."

"But Danny remembers them," Bug said.

"That's because we moved back in with them before you were born," Mama said.

"They finally came around?" Bug asked. Like Lucinda had after Lily had been kidnapped, and she and Holden had joined forces.

"It's more that Aunt Teri stepped in."

"Aunt Teri?" Bug asked. "She was still talking to you?"

Mama nodded. "Yes. She would come to see us even though she now had to sneak."

"Did she like my father?"

"No. But she loved me. And she loved you and your brother. And when Daniel died . . ." Mama paused to clear her throat. "Teri convinced my parents to let us live with them until we got back on our feet."

"So what happened?"

"I'm getting to that." Mama took another deep breath. "We moved back in with my parents. It was awful, but everything was awful back then. And then you came out wailing, fighting from your first breath." A tear fell down Mama's face. "And it seemed like things might be okay. I had you and your brother and help watching you. I thought maybe I could finish school. Become a reporter. Shine a light on important things. But then, when you were about three months old, my parents sat me down for a talk."

A knot twisted in Bug's stomach. She knew that getting sat down for a talk was never good. "What about?"

Mama grimaced, as if in pain. "Baby, I don't want to tell you the rest." She paused. "One day, but not yet."

"Why not?" Bug cried.

"Because the world is as full of love as it is hate. And I want you to marinate in the love a little longer before you see the other side."

"That's not fair!" Bug cried. "I already know it's something bad, and if you don't tell me, it's going to make it worse."

Mama swallowed hard, the way Bug did when she was trying to be brave, trying not to cry. "When you were three months old, my parents offered me a deal."

"A deal?" Bug repeated, knowing that this would not be a good kind of deal—buy one pair of shoes, get a second pair free—but the kind of bad deal Frankie had made. A deal with the devil.

"They said it wasn't too late for me. I could leave behind all that 'unpleasantness.'" Here Mama made finger quotes. "Start fresh." She gulped hard. "They wanted me to annul my marriage to Daniel. Sign a paper that would erase it from the record. This was bad, but I could've forgiven them for that. But then they . . ." Mama trailed off.

"They what?"

Mama put her head in her hands for a minute before stiffening up straight, looking Bug right in the eye. "They wanted me to send your brother away."

"What?" Bug asked. "Send him where?"

"To El Salvador, to be raised by his relatives there. Even though he'd never met them. I'd never met them."

"Why would they want Danny to be raised by strangers?"

"They said it would be easier for me to start over."

"What about me?"

Another tear slid down Mama's face. "You they said I could keep."

Why? Bug was about to ask. But with a sudden sickening feeling, she knew why. Because Danny, even in the baby pictures, looked like their father, and Bug looked like their mother.

It'll be easier for you, Teri had said. *People will treat you differently. Even your own relatives. Even your own grandparents.*

"Why would they do that?" Bug gasped.

"In their mind, I suppose they hoped I would get remarried, to a white man this time, start fresh."

"But without Danny?" Bug felt like throwing up.

Mama's face slackened, the way it always did when she talked about Bug's father. But Bug realized it wasn't Bug's father that made her sad. It was *Mama's* parents.

"I walked out of that house with you and your brother, nowhere to go, no money, no job, halfway through my degree. I didn't know what was going to become of us, but I knew I couldn't stay in that house a moment longer."

"What happened?" Bug asked.

"Aunt Teri happened." Mama gestured toward the bathroom, where her aunt was singing in an off-key voice.

"Aunt Teri?"

Mama nodded. "You know that car she talks about?"

"The cherry-red Mustang?"

"She'd scrimped and saved to buy it and fix it up, and everyone knew it was her when she drove down Mooney Boulevard. She was constantly getting offers from people who wanted to buy it, but that car was her pride and joy. It was her baby. But she sold it."

It took a minute for Bug to understand. "She sold the car? For you?"

"For us," Mama said. "She gave me the money, and we used it to come down here and start over."

"And that's when you took the Greyhound to L.A.?"

Mama nodded.

"No wonder you were crying!"

Mama nodded again.

"Now I understand why we don't have any other family."

This time Mama shook her head. "Oh, but baby, we do." She pointed upstairs to Phillip's apartment. Downstairs to Hedvig's. "It's just a different kind of family."

Citizen's Arrest

THREE THINGS HAPPENED the next day.

The Midnight Marauder struck again, only this time, the victim survived and described him in detail.

There was now a police sketch of what he looked like all over the news. The image looked nothing like the Hermit.

Hedvig returned from Dallas, and Aunt Teri went back to Visalia.

Bug wasn't sure if she was going back because of Hedvig or because of what she'd sort of told Bug. There'd been no fight, but Bug knew Mama was upset with her aunt. At the same time, she was also starting to understand how Mama could be angry at Aunt Teri and still love her. After all, Mama was the one who always said that people were complicated.

The third thing was that Frankie confirmed that Bug was right about the skinheads.

"How do you know?" In all the tumult of the previous day, Bug had not asked Mama about this. Or maybe she hadn't really wanted to know.

"I asked Phillip," Frankie replied, as the two of them played tetherball back at the empty playground.

"And he just told you." Bug thwacked the ball.

"He just told me." Frankie thwacked it back.

"Then why aren't we going to the police?" Bug asked.

"The police already know."

"Are they going to arrest the skinheads?"

Frankie paused before palming the ball back. "They aren't going to arrest anyone."

"Why not?" Bug passed the ball back.

"Probably because they think Phillip deserved it." Frankie held the ball so tightly his knuckles bulged.

Bug was confused. Bad guys had committed a crime. The police knew. Now they would go to jail. That was how it worked, she told Frankie.

"Not in this case," Frankie said. "They aren't doing anything."

Bug was indignant. "They *have* to! I'll call Mama. She'll make the mayor arrest them. He's the boss of the police, and he can make them arrest anyone."

Frankie shook his head. "Phillip doesn't want that. He's afraid if he makes too big of a stink, the families he teaches piano to will find out."

"So?"

"So they'll fire him and then he won't have a job."

Bug was about to say this was silly, but then she thought of Aunt Teri, who believed Phillip deserved getting beaten up. She thought of what Flo said about police paying all that attention to the Midnight Marauder while ignoring attacks on people like them.

"There has to be something we can do," Bug cried. Because this was beyond unfair. She and Frankie had figured out who had attacked Phillip. They'd done it! And now it didn't even matter.

"I've been thinking about that," Frankie replied. "We could do a citizen's arrest."

"A what?"

"It's something people on TV do," Frankie replied. "Like when ordinary people arrest bad guys until the police arrive."

"You want to do a citizen's arrest?" Bug asked, incredulous. "Of the skinheads?"

"Uh-huh," Frankie replied. "I do."

"Are you nuts?" Bug asked. "The skinheads are mean and scary and they beat people up for fun, and anyhow it wouldn't do any good because you do a citizen's arrest until the police arrive, but the police won't come because they don't care. You said so yourself!"

Frankie dribbled against the ball with his fingertips. "That's why we have to do it," he said at last. "So they know we know. So they know they didn't get away with it."

"But they did get away with it," Bug replied. "And a couple of dumb kids telling them otherwise won't change that."

A slow flush crept up Frankie's neck but he didn't say anything. He just let go of the ball and began to walk away.

Bug ran after him. "Where are you going?"

"To find the skinheads."

"How? You don't even know where they are."

"I'll ask."

"What, you're going to ask Randy or Flo? You think they're going to tell you? They know how dangerous guys like that are, even if you don't."

Frankie swiveled to face her. "You think I don't know how dangerous guys like that are?" His eyes blazed. "I might be a *dumb kid*, but trust me, I know."

She watched Frankie, the bravest person she knew, march away. She did not want to go with him. There was nothing in the world that scared Bug more than the skinheads. Not serial killers or earthquakes or big waves, or octopuses hiding in the closet. But Frankie was going to confront them, and he was her best friend, and rule number four still mattered.

The abandoned lifeguard tower was far, maybe a half mile past Tower 19. As she and Frankie walked on the boardwalk past Banana-Boated sunbathers flipping their bodies to catch the best rays of late-summer sun, past Frisbee players skimming their disks across the water, past little kids building sand castles, Bug felt like she was floating above it all. Once upon a time, she had been just like all these people on the beach. And now she wasn't.

At the end of the boardwalk, the sand gave way to a spit of gravel at the narrow mouth of the marina. She saw the hollowed-out lifeguard station in the distance, looking scarier than any Hermit House. Maybe the skinheads wouldn't be there, she hoped. Maybe she and Frankie would come all this way to find an empty lifeguard station.

But then she saw the flash of sunshine reflecting against

metal. They were there. She counted six of them, two of whom Bug recognized from the day at the diner. They were passing around a bottle of something in a paper bag and didn't notice them as Frankie marched right up to the tower, his hands planted resolutely hands on hips.

Bug remained several paces away, her feet refusing to go farther. It was as if the beach was made of quicksand.

Frankie cleared his throat, and the skinheads finally noticed him. "You lost or something?" one asked.

"I'm not lost," Frankie said, but his voice cracked halfway through the sentence. He cleared his throat again. "I'm here . . ." His voice broke off once more. He cleared his throat a third time. "I'm here to make a citizen's arrest."

"A what now?" another skinhead asked. This one had hair so short Bug could see the black cross-in-circle tattoo on his scalp.

"A citizen's arrest," Frankie repeated. "For assault and battery."

Assault and battery. Bug was impressed by that. It sounded official.

"What's he on about?" asked another one.

"I'm talking about my uncle," Frankie replied. "Who you beat up."

"We beat up a lot of people," another skinhead said. "You gotta be more specific." Then he laughed. Like beating up too many people to keep them all straight was the funniest thing in the world.

"You beat up my uncle on August fourteenth outside a bar known as Roosterfish. You broke his ribs, collapsed his lung, and knocked out his tooth. And because of that, we are placing you under a citizen's arrest."

"Roosterfish?" one of the other skinheads said.

"Oh, wait, that's the bar for—" another said, using a word that Bug knew was awful even before she understood that it was a hateful word to describe people like Phillip.

"Don't use that word!" Frankie said.

"Why? You one too?" asked the skinhead with the tattoo on his scalp.

At this, the rest of them started to laugh. The sound of their jeering sent a shock wave of indignation through Bug. How dare they laugh at Frankie! Who had come on an airplane across the country to spend the summer with people he'd never met! Who had roller-skated past the Hermit House! Who had faced the mighty waves of the Pacific head-on! Who had to fight just to be who he was!

Her anger catapulted her out of the quicksand and to her friend's side. "Don't you laugh at him!" she shouted at the skinheads. "He might be a kid, but he's a million times braver than any of you will ever be."

"Is that right?" asked the one with the skull tattoo.

"Yeah! You act all tough, but deep down you're weak. Only weak people have to beat up on innocent people like Phillip."

"Wait, do I know you?" asked one of the other skinheads.

"My name is Beatrice Contreras," Bug replied. "My brother is Daniel Contreras."

"Contreras?" the skinhead repeated. "Is that Mexican?"

"It's Salvadoran! *I'm* Salvadoran. Descended from the mighty Aztecs." She paused, her heart doing cartwheels in her chest as she thought of her father, who had spent his too-short life fighting for justice, who had named her Bug, who never got to meet her was but was a part of her no matter what she looked like. She reached over to grab Frankie's hand. He squeezed back so tightly she heard her knuckles crack. "And this is my best friend, Frankie, and we're doing a citizen's arrest."

"Oh yeah?" The skinhead with the scalp tattoo hopped down from the tower and put his hands together. "Where are your handcuffs?"

Frankie and Bug looked at each other. Neither one of them had really thought this part through. Which became apparent when the rest of the skinheads leapt off the tower and began circling them.

"What now?" Bug whispered to Frankie.

"Now we run," Frankie whispered back.

The two of them took off down the beach, the roar of the ocean and the wind and their own fear and bravery drowning out everything else. They ran hand in hand across the beach, sand churning under them, toward the boardwalk. They ran with all the strength in them, never letting go, staying together always, until, there on the boardwalk, they saw the unmistakable shock of Flo's pink wig, heard the heavy bass beat of Zeus's boom box.

There was a whole group of them, skating, dancing, boogying down the boardwalk to the Rick James song "Super Freak."

Frankie and Bug plunged into the melee and suddenly they were surrounded by voices, laughter, music. Bug wasn't sure if the skinheads were still chasing them, if they had chased them at all. All she knew was that here, surrounded by the bodybuilders and the skaters and the queers and all the superfreaks and refugees who made Venice home, she and Frankie were safe.

Bomb Pops

BUG AND FRANKIE MADE A VOW not to tell anyone about their citizen's arrest. For one, it would get them into so much trouble! Or at the very least, a lot of talking-tos. And in the days that followed Mama telling Bug about Bug's grandparents and Phillip telling Frankie about the skinheads, there had been so many boring family meetings to process everyone's feelings. Frankie and Bug agreed they'd had enough. There were too few precious days of summer to spend them indoors, talking.

During all the meetings, Bug kept looking for ways to ask about Frankie staying in Venice for good, but the time never seemed right to approach Mama. But then she realized it wasn't Mama she needed to ask, so one night while Frankie was helping

Danny and Whitney build a skateboard ramp, Bug made her way up to Phillip's apartment.

He was playing the piano, smiling, looking more like himself.

"Can Frankie stay here? In Venice?" she blurted.

Phillip stopped playing. "That would be nice," he said, and hope filled Bug's chest like a balloon until he added, "but he has his own home."

"Some home," Bug fumed. "His parents are horrible!"

"Oh, I didn't realize you'd met them," Phillip replied, his mustache twitching in amusement.

"You know I haven't," Bug replied. "They have to be horrible to make Frankie be someone he isn't."

Phillip nodded, like maybe he was agreeing. Then he said, "Did you ever think about why my sister sent Frankie here?"

"To get it out of his system."

"Little strange to send Frankie to live with his gay uncle to get it out of his system."

It was the first time Phillip had ever referred to himself as gay in front of Bug. Her face must've registered shock because Phillip smiled. "I'm gay, Beatrice. I know I've kept this part of my life separate from you, but I want you to know, I love who I am, I love my life, even with . . ." He gestured to his eye where the bruise was already starting to fade. "And I love Frankie and want Frankie to love his life too." He paused once more. "I believe my sister wants that for him too."

"But then why make Frankie go home and be someone he isn't?"

"No one can make Frankie be someone he isn't. Frankie is who Frankie is."

"But what about the deal? Frankie's father? Who thinks he's a mistake?"

Phillip shrugged. "Life is long. And people are complicated."

Bug thought of Aunt Teri, who had said terrible things about her father and Phillip but had sold her cherry-red Mustang to help Mama come to Venice. She didn't know if Phillip was right. But she sure hoped he was.

"I was hoping if we caught Phillip's attacker, Mama and Phillip would be so grateful that they'd let you stay," Bug told Frankie later that night as the two of them sat on the curb outside Dixon's, eating Bomb Pops as they watched Danny and Whitney do skateboard tricks on their newly constructed ramp. "If that's what you wanted," Bug added.

"I have to go home," Frankie said. "You can have my wet suit, if you want."

"I don't need a wet suit. I can handle the cold water. I'm tough."

"I know you are," Frankie said.

There was a kind of tough that could swim in the cold Pacific, and then there was the kind of tough Frankie was.

"Are you scared?" Bug asked. "To go home?"

Frankie didn't reply at first, just slowly licked. The Bomb Pops were cherry on top, lemon in the middle, and blue raspberry on the bottom. Frankie liked red best, so he ate the top part the most slowly. Bug liked the blue, so she hurried through red and white to get to it.

"It's home," Frankie said, as if that answered the question.

"But aren't the people there . . ." Bug trailed off, thinking of what Phillip had said about Frankie's mom.

"Mean?" Frankie finished.

Bug nodded.

"There are nice people and mean people everywhere."

Bug thought of Venice. On one hand, there were people like Phillip and Hedvig and Randy and Duane and Flo, but on the other hand, the skinheads.

"Too bad we didn't catch the Midnight Marauder," Frankie said.

Frankie finished the red part of his Bomb Pop and let the white drip all over his hands. It occurred to Bug that they could've devised a system, Bug trading him the red part of hers for the blue part of his. But now it was too late. He was leaving. She would probably never see him again.

She shivered, the ice of the pop invading her veins, suddenly overcome by a terrible sadness, as if it wasn't just *this* summer that was ending but *all* summers.

There was so much she wanted to say to him, but her throat was thick with pent-up tears. She knew crying in front of him would only make Frankie feel bad too. So she swallowed and said, "Yeah, I wish we'd caught him too."

"But at least we caught the skinheads," Frankie said.

And it was a funny thing, because Bug had been right: citizen-arresting the skinheads hadn't really changed anything. Except Frankie seemed to walk a little taller and Bug kept imagining her father being proud of what she'd done, and it made her feel a little closer to him, somehow. So maybe it *had* changed something.

"At least we caught the skinheads," Bug replied.

This time, they all went to the airport: Frankie and Bug and Mama and Phillip and Danny and Hedvig, all squashed into the Datsun. They walked Frankie through the terminal to the gate.

"Here," Hedvig said, handing Frankie a dirty Tupperware full of who knew what. "Food for the flight." Though Phillip had already made Frankie two pastrami sandwiches, Frankie accepted the Tupperware with a grateful smile.

"Do you know that in my Magyar, my language," Hedvig said, "we have no, how you call it, pronouns for boy or girl. It is the same for he or she."

"Really?" Frankie asked.

"Really," Hedvig said, and hugged him. Then Mama did, and Phillip. Danny shook his hand using the complicated high-five handshake he and the guys at Muscle Beach often exchanged but which he'd never deigned to use with Frankie or Bug.

Finally, Frankie turned to Bug. "I have something for you," he said in a raspy voice. He pulled out his Los Angeles map, now coming apart at the creases, and handed it to Bug. "You're a really good detective."

"So are you," she said, swallowing the giant lump in her throat. "I have something for you, too." She opened a small box to reveal the grain of rice she'd had inscribed with their names: *Frankie & Bug*. It was so small she thought he could keep being Frankie and his family would never have to know. But *he'd* know.

When Frankie's flight was starting to board, he turned to Bug and pulled her to him. He was shaking. Or maybe she was. It was hard to tell where one ended and the other began. They held on to each other until Phillip said gently, "Frankie, it's time."

Phillip walked him to the gate, whispering something into his ear. Frankie nodded solemnly, and, shooting one more look Bug's way, disappeared onto the jet bridge.

"I want to watch him take off," Bug said.

Phillip nodded. "If it's all right by you, I'm going to take a rest."

"I'll go with you," Hedvig said.

"Me too," Danny said.

Bug and Mama walked over to the window and watched as the jet bridge was pulled back, and the plane was pushed away from the gate. When the engines roared to life, all the emotions Bug had been holding back exploded into a great gust of tears.

Mama stayed quiet, just rubbing Bug's back until she stopped crying. "We'll all miss him," Mama said in a soft voice.

Bug sniffed. She *would* miss Frankie. So much. But that wasn't the only reason she was crying. She didn't even *know* why she was crying. She understood now what Hedvig had meant about being a refugee. She believed what Phillip said about loving his life, and that no one could turn Frankie into someone he wasn't, but why, then, did Frankie leaving make Bug feel not just sad, but mad?

She knew she was only ten, but she was so tired of other people making all the rules!

"You always say that life isn't fair, that the best we can hope for is that it's just. But how is what happened to Phillip just? How is what's going to happen to Frankie just?"

Mama was quiet for so long Bug thought maybe she wouldn't answer. She looked back out the window. Frankie's plane was third in the takeoff line when Mama finally spoke. "Sometimes justice takes time."

Bug exhaled a shuddery sigh. "Why do grown-ups always say that? Don't you know how hard it is to wait?"

Mama nodded slowly. "Maybe we forget." She turned toward the runway. Frankie's plane was now second in line. "Thanks for reminding me. And for reminding me that it's up to all of us to hurry toward justice." She looked at Bug. "Sometimes you lose sight of that."

Frankie's plane was now at the front of the takeoff line. As Bug watched it accelerate down the runway, her tears dried as her sadness lifted into something else, something warm and deep inside: a promise to herself, to Frankie, to do whatever she could to, as Mama had said, hurry toward justice.

Frankie's plane rose into the air. It would, Bug knew, fly out over the Pacific Ocean before banking inland and taking him home.

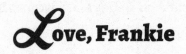

ℒove, Frankie

A WEEK AFTER FRANKIE LEFT, the Midnight Marauder was caught. He'd gone to Boise, Idaho, and then ridden back to L.A. on a Greyhound bus. He was captured not far from the station.

In the end, it wasn't the police who got him, but citizens who recognized him and chased him down, subduing him until the cops arrived.

This made Bug happy. She wondered if it made Frankie happy too.

A few days later, she got her answer when the first letter from Frankie arrived.

A citizen's arrest! he wrote. *And at the bus station. Wasn't that where you picked your aunt up? I bet she never comes to visit you again. If you're lucky! Haha.*

Bug had not told Frankie the whole story about Aunt Teri, who had been so hateful to Phillip and Bug's father but had also sold her cherry-red Mustang so Mama could come to Venice and make a new family, one that included Hedvig and Phillip and now Frankie, too. But she would tell him that in her first letter back, along with all her other news, like how she didn't play with Beth Ann at recess anymore, but she'd made a new friend at school named Paco, who had also followed the Midnight Marauder case and who was going to help her practice Spanish now that she was taking lessons too. When the war ended in El Salvador, Mama promised they would all go there to see where Bug and Daniel and their father came from.

Bug continued reading Frankie's letter. There was nothing about how it was to be home. Or about the deal. Everything was about the Midnight Marauder.

Except for the last two lines of the letter.

Because after he signed off, Frankie added the following postscript.

PS: Don't get rid of my wet suit. I'm already bugging my mom to let me come back next summer!

And right above that, in the blockish scrawl that would become so familiar to Bug over the years, the letter was signed with the only name Bug would ever know her best friend as, the person he was—the person he would always be.

The letter was signed: *Love, Frankie.*

Ackowledgments

ONE OF THE THEMES OF *Frankie & Bug* is finding the place in the world where you belong. With that in mind, I begin my thank-you with my editor, Kristin Gilson. This special book, these special children, needed to find their home. And that home was with you.

Thank you to everyone at Aladdin and Simon & Schuster who embraced these kids with such love and enthusiasm: Mara Anastas, Jon Anderson, Savannah Breckenridge, Valeria Garfield, Lauren Hoffman, Anna Jarzab, Amelia Jenkins, Michelle Leo, Cassie Malmo, Elizabeth Mims, Chelsea Morgan, Beth Parker, Nicole Russo, Caitlin Sweeny, Erin Toller, Rebecca Vitkus, and Sarah Woodruff. A special thank-you to Laura DiSiena and

Angeles Ruiz for the gorgeous, pitch-perfect cover, and also to Laura for the interior.

As a white cisgender woman writing about a biracial kid and a trans kid, I required lots of help. Isabel Bermúdez Kyriacou has been one of my best friends, my Salvadoreña sister, for more than a decade, and it was my honor to funnel so many of her stories and experiences, not to mention the culinary treats of pupusas and curtido, into this story. Gracias por tu amistad, mi amor. Te amo.

Devon Shanley was my first sensitivity read for *Frankie & Bug*, and he shaped the book—and me—in innumerable ways, making me think deeply about my own blind spots and stereotypes and also really look at what it means to stand up for someone in the way they need you to, not the way you want to. Devon made this book deeper, and better, and I like to think he did the same for me.

Thank you to Clay Hobson, Noa Kleiman, and all my children's friends and their peers, who, like so many young people today, are blowing up our ideas of how gender should be performed.

Thank you to the Varga clan, Hedy, Maria, Laslzo, and Mark for inspiring Hedvig's story, not to mention the Venice apartment building where the book is set.

Thank you to the legions of friends and readers who have

championed this book over the years and helped get it to where it now is: Michael Bourret, Libba Bray, Christa Desir, Adam Gidwitz, Tamara Glenny, Molly Ker Hawn, Marjorie Ingall, Raquel Jaramillo, Emily Jenkins, Courtney Sheinmel, Jacqueline Woodson, and Kieryn Ziegler.

Thank you, Team New Leaf: Meredith Barnes, Katherine Curtis, Veronica Grijalva, Victoria Hendersen, Hilary Pecheone, Dani Segelbaum, Pouya Shahbazian, Kate Sullivan, Jo Volpe, and last but definitely not least, the wonderful Suzie Townsend.

Thank you to the wonderful booksellers, librarians, and educators who have put my books in the hands of readers for more than a decade now. Thank you for taking the leap with me into middle-grade!

Thank you to my family, the one I was born into and the one I created. I love you all.

And finally, I want to thank all the young people who have read this book . . . all the way to the last paragraph of the acknowledgments, no less. You are the reason this book exists. You have the power to change a life, and in doing so, to change the world. Never forget that.

Resources

If you'd like to learn more about refugees and why they leave home, and what happens to them after they leave, here are some resources.

Facing History (facinghistory.org) has excellent resources for educators and students that examine the link between discrimination and hatred now and what happened in the past, with content particular to the proxy wars in Central America and how that has led to the current refugee crisis.

For information/resources specific to immigrants' rights or for those in need of legal support, contact the Refugee and Immigrant Center for Education and Legal Services (RAICES) at raicestexas.org.

The International Rescue Committee (rescue.org) has information about crises that force families to flee their homes, and also provides support.

Doctors Without Borders, also known as Médecins Sans Frontières (doctorswithoutborders.org), is a great resource for country-specific news about refugee (and other) crises around the world from medical professionals who are in the trenches.

Gringolandia by Lyn Miller-Lachmann is a young-adult novel about an immigrant teen boy living the American dream in Wisconsin coming to terms what happened to his political-prisoner father after he's released.

The wonderful graphic novel *When Stars Are Scattered* by Victoria Jamieson and Omar Mohamed is about African, not Central American, refugees, but the way it beautifully captures the life of young refugees is universal.

Resources for trans/nonbinary/ gender-nonconforming kids and their families

The go-to place for support for LGBTQ+ people, GLAAD (glaad .org/transgender/resources), has tons of information for young people and their families and is a great first step for anyone questioning their gender identity and for families seeking to understand a gender-nonconforming child.

Trans Lifeline [(877) 565-8860; translifeline.org] is a grass-roots hotline offering direct emotional and financial support to trans people in crisis—for the trans community, by the trans community.

If you are a young person in crisis, are feeling suicidal, or are in need of a safe and judgment-free place to talk, call the Trevor Project's TrevorLifeline now at 1-866-488-7386.

The Human Rights Campaign (hrc.org/resources/transgender -children-and-youth-understanding-the-basics) has been fight-ing for LGBTQ+ rights for decades, and its website contains a wealth of information for trans kids and their families, including a primer on trans issues and up-to-date medical resources.

The Trans Youth Equality Foundation (transyouthequality.org) has, among other things, an excellent reading guide for children of all ages. A great resource for kids, families, and educators!

As its name suggests, TransFamilies (transfamilies.org) is an organization to support families of trans kids and the kids themselves. It runs virtual parent support groups in English and Spanish, and a trans youth leadership program. Programs are online, available for families everywhere.

Author's Note

The first time I understood the word "gay," I was probably around thirteen years old. My sister brought home a friend—let's call him Kelly—who was, I thought, the nicest, coolest, best-smelling human in the world. He was so lovely to me, and I adored him. The thought that anyone would not love Kelly because of who Kelly loved made no sense to me.

A few years later when the AIDS epidemic hit crisis proportions, I began volunteering for AIDS Project Los Angeles. I worked at a food bank, preparing shopping bags full of food for men who could no longer shop for themselves.

By then, I was well aware of the homophobia rampant in the country. Elected leaders refused to even say the word "AIDS," let alone do anything about it. Religious leaders said gay men stricken with AIDS were receiving God's wrath. I didn't understand this vitriol at all. How could anyone *deserve* sickness? Who cared who someone loved? What did it cost you to let someone be themselves?

Around the time that AIDS was ravaging a generation of gay men, wars were also destroying lives in Latin America. In countries like El Salvador, Nicaragua, and Chile, repressive governments clamped down on dissidents for simply speaking out against the government or organizing a union, using chilling tactics including torture, disappearances, and murder. Often this happened with the United States government's support because these countries were fighting so-called proxy wars during the Cold War between the United States and the Soviet Union. Many, many people were killed in these wars, but some did escape, to the United States, even. The story of Bug's father fleeing the government and taking refuge in the United States is taken directly from my friend Isabel's grandmother.

The seed of *Frankie & Bug* was inspired by the idea that the world can change with breathtaking speed, and wrongs can be righted in ways unimaginable. And at the same time, the world can also stay stubbornly the same, repeating its wrongs in new ways. If I could fly back in time to the 1980s and tell Kelly what his future might look like, would he believe me? In much of the world, AIDS has gone from a death sentence to a chronic manageable disease. Justice is not a destination, and there is much work to be done, but it is also true that LGBTQ rights have taken leaps forward since the 1980s. Marriage equality, same-sex parents, gay/lesbian rom-coms: these were inconceivable decades ago; now they are commonplace.

And yet, at the same time, transphobia is on the rise, with states passing laws dictating who can use what bathroom and who can play on what team, barring families from making personal medical decisions. Some of the ugly transphobic rhetoric sounds chillingly familiar to the homophobia of the 1980s when gays and lesbians were accused of being a "threat" to straight people. It made no sense then. It makes no sense now. And again, I go back to the question: What does it cost you to let someone else be who they are? To love who they want?

Today, different battles rage in Central America, where violent crime runs rampant (in part because of the ravages left by the proxy wars of the 1960s–1980s). This has pushed a new generation of refugees to leave home in search of safety. In 2021, when the charity Doctors Without Borders interviewed refugees from El Salvador and Guatemala, it found that 42.5 percent of interviewees reported the violent death of a relative over the previous two years, while 16.2 percent had had a relative forcibly disappeared, and 9.2 percent had a loved one kidnapped. Stop and think about that. Nearly half the people witnessed a loved one being killed! *This* is what motivated them to flee to the United States. But again, we see rhetoric, from politicians, from the media, villainizing refugees as criminals or terrorists. They are not. They are human beings, seeking a safe harbor in the United States, like so many generations before them.

As I wrote this book, I thought of this quote from Dr. Martin Luther King Jr.: "The arc of the moral universe is long, but it bends toward justice."

What that means is that change can take a long time, but things do, eventually, change for the better, even if sometimes it seems like for every step forward, there is one backward. What it doesn't mean is that we can all kick up our heels and just wait. "Hope" is a verb, something you dream of, and work for. "Ally" is a verb, something you become by showing up, doing the work. It's up to all of us to hope, to ally, and as Bug's mother says, to hurry toward justice.

Maybe you, young readers, don't need to hear this. Sometimes

I think you get this more than the rest of us, the inherent tenets of fairness, justice, equity. And that's why I wrote this book. To honor what you already know. To validate what you are trying to teach us. And to remind you that you can change the world. You already are.

About the Author

AWARD-WINNING AUTHOR and journalist Gayle Forman (she/her) has written several bestselling novels, including *I Have Lost My Way*, *Leave Me*, the Just One series, and the number one New York Times bestseller *If I Stay*, which has been translated into more than forty languages and in 2014 was adapted into a major motion picture. Gayle's essays and nonfiction work have appeared in publications like the *New York Times*, *Elle*, the *Nation*, and *Time*. She lives in Brooklyn, New York, with her family.